Death Metal Epic II

GOAT SONG SACRIFICE

Dean Swinford

ATLATL

Atlatl Press
POB 293161
Dayton, Ohio 45429
atlatlpress.com

Death Metal Epic (Book Two: Goat Song Sacrifice)
Copyright © 2017 by Dean Swinford
Cover design copyright © 2017 by Matthew Revert
Author photo courtesy of James Olon Archive
ISBN-13: 978-1-941918-16-6
ISBN-10: 1-941918-16-6

Infernal Praise for the Death Metal Epic

"A superb first book in what will hopefully end up being the definitive trilogy about death metal."
—*Verbicide*

"A bloody good read. Swinford's style is bold and original, his characters full of depth and intrigue, and come the end, you'll be chomping at the bit for the next installment." (4 stars)
—*Terrorizer*

"Helps define the nature of metal at the fringes."
—*Metal Music Studies*

"Fits squarely in the tradition of such now classics as Joe Meno's *Hairstyles of the Damned* or Abram Shalom Himelstein's *Tales of a Punk Rock Nothing*; a plain-spoken and moving ode to outsider art and its transformative effect."
—CCLaP: Chicago Center for Literature and Photography

Also by Dean Swinford

Fiction

Death Metal Epic (Book One: The Inverted Katabasis)

Criticism

Through the Daemon's Gate: Kepler's Somnium, *Medieval Dream Narratives, and the Polysemy of Allegorical Motifs*

GOAT SONG SACRIFICE

The Second Book

of the

Death Metal Epic

Acknowledgements

Thanks to the following for your help and support: Alison Van Nyhuis, Will Swinford, Reed Swinford, Scott Swinford, Andersen Prunty, C.V. Hunt, Jeff Vrabel, Matt Hinch, Gabino Iglesias, Eric Sanders, Jason Flom, John Isenhour, Jason Pettus, Brett Stevens, Kriscinda Everitt, Mike Kemp, Abel Folgar, Niall Scott, James Ortega, D. Harlan Wilson, James Langston, Duke Matsuyama, Mike Liassides, Jude Felton, Bryan Bardine, Shawn Macomber, Pim Blankenstein, Jeff Jones, Kelly Davis, Tom Dawson, Matthew Revert, and all the bands (too many to list) engaged in the excavation of the eternal and ever-changing goat song.

Table of Contents

Part Three

The hammer breaks metal, and the fire melts it.
—John Lydgate, *The Fall of Princes*

I believe in tragedies,
I believe in desecration.
—Immortal, "The Sun No Longer Rises"

1.
Metametal: Kvlt ov Nekro

Obscure signs mark the Nekronomikon's pages, each brittle leaf a vast forest of forbidden knowledge, each letter obscure in its shape, its sound, its incarnadined hue.

Once the true penitent has enacted the ritual necessary to locate the hidden book, floated through a living tunnel of twined branches connected, at the roots, to the book's source, and severed the book's sacred pages with sacred steel, once the true penitent has done these things, the arduous task of severing its sacred meaning from its sacred signs remains and, beyond that,

beyond the forest that, in one telling, holds and is the book,

beyond the tower that, in another, conceals the crone who creates and destroys the book again and again as the book creates and destroys her,

beyond the very ocean that, in a third, contains the host of beasts, the scaled armor of each engraved with a letter, the message of the book eternally configured and reconfigured as these beasts, these letters, swarm in the depths,

beyond these and all other physical traces of the Nekronomikon,

one act remains: the act of invoking its hidden words and pronouncing in human speech a message that precedes and subsumes all that is human.

The sound of the Nekronomikon's word is death and the penitent who speaks the words speaks death, speaks nekro, the transcendent message of total death spoken by a living corpse, one living, who is, who once never was, and who, at some point, will never be again.

The penitent recites, in whole or part, it makes no difference, for a single character of that book encompasses its message, and its message can only be conveyed through a total recitation recited in total by all that lives and dies, an eternal message in fading breath.

The path to the Nekronomikon remains clearest in a forest obscured by fog, the very breath of its trees, and in a song obscured by hiss, the very sign of its transitory impermanence.

2.
Ik Ben Heel Mooi

Svart liked to drink. J. Svart. Jurgen Svart. A paunchy man-mountain, solid metal to the core. Sometimes I called him Svartikles.

He worked at the Record Huis, remember?

And when he wasn't clocked in there, he masterminded Desekration's impending blasphemation of little baby Jesus, our unrecorded and unwritten opus diabolicum, *Infernö*. The album remained unrecorded because, according to Svart, I was still in training. Not quite ready to contribute to "the forthcoming masterwork." That's what he called it.

Also, we spent most of our time drinking. Svart liked to drink. A lot. And curse, too.

Mainly in Dutch, but not exclusively. He was a regular polyglot. "Vooruit," or "progress," may have been my first word in a new language, but I quickly added essential terms like "verdomme," "klootzak," and "pokkelijder" to my repertoire.

During the day, dude was nearly silent. Like most Belgians. A Gent street could be filled with people, cars, buses, but if you closed your eyes, you'd never know. You'd think you were alone in the countryside with nothing but a well-oiled windmill for company.

A well-oiled Svart got loud. Full of opinions. Mostly about music, about the superlative merits of the poorly produced buzz-saw black metal he had me listening to daily. When I woke up, the thud of my morning hangover kept time with the repetitive barrage of the Bathory and Celtic Frost LPs he spun on his ancient turntable. And every night, the same tunes lulled me into a drunken slumber on the pink and white floral patterned couch in the living room of his mom's house.

Mostly about music, but not always. His pronouncements were just as likely to assess whatever semi-attractive girl had the bad fortune to walk past him, three drinks down the gullet.

The first time he took me to the goth pub by his house, he motioned to the pierced, leather-clad bartendress and said, "You see that girl's lip ring? Like a fishing hook." Then he grabbed his crotch. "One time, I reel her in with this veiny worm. Ha ha!"

And another night when a thirty-something jogger in running tights sprinted down the street, he turned to me and said, "Verdomme, that's one athletic bitch." He waggled his belly fat. "You think she'll help me train? Ha ha!"

That was my regimen for the first month or so after I joined his band. After the epic Eurotour of my former band, Katabasis, shattered into a million puppet shards and I left Juan, my former bandmate, fellow American, and onetime friend, standing in the middle of Sint Baafsplein, a city square in the medieval heart of my new home, Gent.

Once I'd explained my tenuous money situation to Svart, he took me in. Showed me the beauty of the Belgian summer. Under Svart's wing, I lived the Eurometal life to the hilt, and the city's endless festivals and outdoor beer gardens flowed together into a single, unending ale-drenched day punctuated by inebriated couch flops.

I did not miss Juan. I did not miss home. I did not miss that dreaded pink bedroom, crammed with my stuff, waiting for me somewhere in the miasmal reaches of Miami's far-flung suburbs.

I didn't miss Juan, but I saw him the night Svart and I went to meet a drummer for our group. We hadn't been out too long. First, we had a drink at the goth pub so we could leer at the bartendress. She wasn't there, so we came up to the main student party drag, called Overpoortstraat, to go to Svart's favorite doner kebab place. We stood on the sidewalk, shoveling friets into our mouths as we watched the flow of Gent nightlife.

"Eat up, my friend," he said, "We're just getting started."

The creamy grout of Svart's andalouse-sauce fries spackled his chin as he chewed. I heard a familiar voice—a high pitched squeal, unmistakably Juan—coming from the street, where a line of bicyclists filed through an intersection. I looked up reflexively. I hadn't seen him since a tram killed his puppet. Since I threw a puppet he bought for his girlfriend Delphine in front of a tram, then left him so he couldn't waste my ultralimited cash flow on any other stupid toys. That squeal—it had to be Juan—was the same exultant noise he used in those early months, a long, high "what's up?" as I crossed the university parking lot to go to the campus studio where we recorded *In Circle of Ouroboros*, or a loud "you've got to hear this!" as he burst into the Crown and Garter, my Coral Gables drinking hole, with a tape of something he'd recorded without me. Besides, if I'd learned anything under Svart's tutelage, it was that no Belgian—male or female—could produce such a noise—high, loud, and enthusiastic.

Except, if you believed Svart, the leather-clad bartendress last summer during one long lost night of burning passion on the couch I called home. "No lie," he'd told me. "That stain on your pillow, that's my jizz. My mom, she thinks it's hot cocoa. Ha ha!"

Among the bike herd spinning down the street, I made out Delphine's trollish figure and, drafting in the ample air-free bubble behind her, Juan, a beatific smile on his face, his moccasin fringes wiggling wildly as he pedaled. They zoomed past; I held up my frietfork, a tiny, two tined beacon, his name on the tip of my tongue, but he didn't see me. I felt like I got a brief and unvarnished glance into his life, the way that the last month had been so good to him.

He didn't ignore me. Nothing—anger, annoyance—creased his face. For that instant, I saw him with no trace of a negative emotion. And then he was gone. A tiny part of me wanted to leap onto Juan's handlebars, or jump onto Delphine's hump of a back, cling to her like a baby monkey. But then Svart's massive craw, chewing, chewing, chewing, inserted itself into my reverie. There was no time for introspection in his company. He shoulder checked me, then pointed at some girl walking the other direction:

"We have a saying. An ass you can set a beer on," he pretended to set his glass on an imaginary, waist high shelf, "and park a bike in. That's the ideal! Ha ha!"

That snapped me out of it. Juan was an asshole. A leech. And Svart's rawness had rubbed off on me. Raw. Crude. A creeping crudity. So I stabbed a fry, stuffed it in my mouth, and said, loud enough for the girl to hear as she speedwalked past, "We have a saying, too: 'My anaconda don't want none unless you got buns, hon!'"

This was the kind of conversation I had with Svart before anyone else joined Desekration. Jockish. Broish. In ways I never acted when I lived in the home of broish jockishness. I felt like a pledge in some metal frat. We did not ponder the undulations of the ouroboros, that long forgotten ancient serpent. Unless by "ancient serpent" one of us, like Sir Mix-A-Lot, meant a dick, and by "undulations" one of us meant some sexual act, pijpen or neuken.

"Ha ha!" He repeated it, committed it to memory. "This I like very much. Come. There's another bar we must go to. We have to meet the new drummer. Finish the frietjes, like I said. You finish because he's Finnish. You ever meet a Finn?"

He shoved another handful in his mouth; in between chews, he said, "I have known a few. I'm sure we will be drinking heavily tonight."

We met the new guy at a bar off the Korenmarkt in the city center. Inside, bookshelves lined the walls, and people sat in pairs playing chess. Upscale. The twisted balloon squeal of free jazz saxophones surged through the place. I spotted him right away. He was the guy with a chess piece in each hand, beating them on the table rim in time with every break, every hummingbird-hearted fill. He had thick, hairless forearms bursting from a tight, almost turtleneck top with elbow-length sleeves. It looked like a wetsuit fashioned out of Lycra. His blond hair was tied back in a ponytail, revealing a long, nearly ovoid forehead. His blond moustache circled around his mouth into an equally round goatee. His head looked like a figure 8 of blond hair woven around the central point of his short, pug nose.

And what Svart said about the drinking? He was right. The guy passed that part of the audition with no competition. He easily outpaced Svart, but the alcohol did not serve as a social lubricant. He introduced himself—Tomi Umunhumunvaari or some related blur of vowels—then settled back in his seat, quietly tapping the chess pieces in time with the music. When the waiter brought the first round, Tomi stopped his drumming, grabbed the glass, and pounded it back. He finished before the foam had even settled in the glass. Then, he flagged down the waiter and repeated the process. By the third time he did this, I knew I was in trouble. Svart felt it was his duty to keep up and he wouldn't let me sip gently at my own pace while he followed Tomi into a chasm of blinding drunkenness. Instead, he'd also order for me, point at my nearly full glass, and say, "Drink up, Captain America. You can do it!"

When Tomi wasn't drinking, he sat quietly. He answered "yes" or "no" to Svart's questions, and occasionally added a few words to elaborate. He moved to Belgium a few months ago after he got married. He worked in landscaping for the city. He had been corresponding with Svart since "To Winds ov Demise" came out. Like Svart, he, too, was sick of death metal, though he admired drummers like Gene Hoglan. What stuck with me was the impression that he could drum like he drank: fast and deliberate without any distractions.

It was a good thing I finished those fries. As a matter of survival. Otherwise, I would have spent the next day languishing on the couch, its little pink flowers drenched in a regurgitated blend of mashed fries, andalouse sauce, and Belgian ale. Or I could have died of alcohol poisoning, drowned on dry land, my brew-logged corpse bloating as the morning sun shone over the Korenmarkt. Instead, I woke up early and headed to a classroom. Head pounding and on the verge of explosive vomiting, but on time and prepared. Svart's mom taught Dutch at a language school connected to the local university. She convinced me to sign up for Dutch niveau een, level one, after a couple weeks of finding me on her couch every morning. She told me it would help me meet girls. "Besides," she added as she gave me a registration form one morning, "the summer's nearly over. As long as you're here, you should try to learn something."

I knew she was right, even though I think by "meeting girls" she really meant maybe I'd find somewhere else to sleep. In class, I sat next to Katrin, a tall brunette from Azerbaijan. She seemed unfazed by the stink of booze wafting from my pores; her perfume neutralized my unpleasant odors. With her firm posture, and even firmer breasts, God knows what Svart would say if he saw her on one of his nightly pub crawls. She was taken, though. Married to some Belgian engineer. Had a college degree in journalism, too. Whenever she said hello and sat next to me, I unslouched. Tucked my hair behind my ears. Tried to act respectable.

The teacher, Helena, started promptly at nine. Every day, she went around the room and asked us all a simple question. Last week, it was "Hoe heet jij?," which means "What's your name?" Once we got that, we advanced to a more complex prompt—"Hoe gaat het?" or "How are you?" This was no American-style pedagogy, though, where every utterance gets treated as some gold-plated gift from on high. If you fucked up, you'd know.

To make matters worse, Helena hated Americans. An acerbic Gent meisje with sharp rodent features and curly brown hair, she looked like a rat chewing through a ball of yarn as she over-enunciated for us foreigners. Most of the time, she'd find some way to ridicule my accent, or pretend to be Keanu Reeves whenever I said anything. Also, she seemed to think the last three decades of US foreign policy rested squarely on my shoulders. When she talked, correcting and imitating our strange legion of garblings, the veins in her neck pulsed as if some endoparasite strained to escape.

Still, I'd get a bit turned on in class. Maybe she mocks me because she wants me? I'd think, my own little ouroboros stirring to life. You could probably blame it on the Azerbrunette's perfume. This was no citrus blast, no floral syrup. A musky atmosphere of Europerfume surrounded her. It didn't Lysol away the scent of the body, but reinforced it, so that, nearly every day, my thoughts strayed from Dutch verb conjugation and fixated instead on that warmest, most bodily female scent. As I breathed in the lush fragrance of some pubic Endor, I'd think of fuzzy Ewoks. I'd think of their little red hoods. I'd think of pussy. Of all the pussy I'd ever encountered. Which meant, and I know this damages my metal credibility, I'd think of the only one I'd really encountered, studied, examined, all up close and personal. I'd think of Natasha, the ex-girlfriend I couldn't quite let go.

When I sensed Katrin straighten up next to me, I came out of my reverie. It was her turn to answer Helena's question, "How are you?" Katrin smiled, and began to speak. That meant I'd be next. I flipped through the chapter. The trick was to use the most recent vocabulary. That way, you created the illusion of progress. Katrin ruled these exercises. She was never ridiculed.

She said, "Ik ben heel gelukkig vandaag. Gisteren, ben ik naar het huisarts gegaan. Ik ben zwanger." The class erupted in applause. Everyone smiled, even Helena, who generally found at least one "fout" or "error" in every answer. This girl, who'd been in Belgium as long as I had, had managed to string together several sentences.

What she'd said was, "I am very happy today. Yesterday, I was at the doctor. I am pregnant."

The applause subsided. All eyes turned to me. The pressure mounted.

"En jij," Helena asked with a sneer, "Hoe gaat het?"

Hungover? We hadn't covered that yet. Maybe in a later chapter—Lesson Nine: The Beers? The closest I could think of was "tired." We covered it in Les Twee, about daily routines. The word came to me. I stretched my arms out, too, like I was yawning. I couldn't speak in long sentences, or even refer to past events. In Dutch, I lived in mythic time. The continuous present.

"Ik ben . . ." I paused, big fake yawn. Might as well throw in an intensifier, too.

"Heel." Very.

"Mooi." Tired.

No applause, just laughter. She gestured, too, one hand on her hip, the other in her hair. She shook her hips. "Mooi? Ben jij heel mooi?" I didn't catch on. Was she flirting with me?

She explained. "Mooi means pretty. You are very pretty?"

"Oh. I meant to say tired. Isn't it . . ."

"Moe." She cut me off, stretching the word out and mimicking a cow. "Mooooo. Moe. Jij bent heel moe, dude."

I told Svart about my gaffe when he got back from work. I was sitting cross-legged on the floor in front of the stereo in the living room, guitar in my lap, plucking along to "Dee," an acoustic song written by virtuoso Randy Rhodes. It's not easy. That guy, a true guitar god, recorded it by overdubbing a couple of guitar tracks. I found *Blizzard of Ozz* wedged between two Molly Hatchet albums in a neglected corner of Svart's record collection and spent most of the afternoon revisiting songs I used to know pretty well in the early Valhalla days. I hadn't really made any friends in class yet.

He didn't laugh. He'd been in a bad mood that morning,

too, but I thought he was simply, like me, struggling through the wretched hangover caused by our night out with Tomi. Svart pursed his lips, then took the needle off the record and muttered, "Ozzy. Hmm. My mom, she likes this one."

I told him again, this time including the part about Katrin, how she was like some freak of nature, some linguistic prodigy, and pregnant too. On track to become a useful Belgian citizen.

Nothing.

"Mooi. En moe." He dragged out each word, just like my Dutch teacher. He said them again, "Mooi. En moe." Loudly. Like I had some kind of impairment.

"They are very different words. Are you not studying?"

What could I say to him? He seemed genuinely upset. That I'd like to study more, but it interfered with my party schedule?

He picked my textbook off the couch and flipped through it. He asked me what chapter we were on. I told him and he plonked his fat finger on the end of unit vocabulary page.

"Stop noodling. I will quiz you."

After we went through the list several times, he sighed, "Godverdomme." I missed half and mispronounced the other half. "Fucking Turks speak better than you. And what is that shit you playing?" I still absentmindedly fingered the strings.

"That's easy listening," he said, then pulled Bathory's *Under the Sign of the Black Mark* off the shelf. The cover looked like a still taken from *Conan the Barbarian*, but with a Xeroxed goat head taped over Arnold Schwarzenegger's face. The rest of the album is not quite as well produced as the cover. I'm no drummer, but even I can tell the tempo shifts wildly at times. I'm no sound engineer, but even I know a listener shouldn't be able to hear the sounds of the lawnmowers and passing traffic outside of the guy's "home studio."

And as a guitarist? I wince when the guy bumbles the riff at least twice per song.

He put it on to some song that starts with the kind of jackhammering Tomi excelled at.

"No more of this!" he said, and slipped *Blizzard* back into its sleeve.

Goodbye, Ozzy!

"Or these either." He hauled a big stack of records from that far corner and stomped to his room.

Before he shut the door, he turned and said, "No party tonight. Dutch language is not the only thing you need to study."

3.
Niveau Een

I sat on the couch. My hands in my lap. Scolded. Guilty. Like I'd forgotten to mow the lawn. Or reeling with shame. Like the time my mom dangled a yellowed sock, a crusted jizz mitt, in my face and asked me to help her, at least just a little bit, by cleaning under my bed without being asked.

Svart never felt that way.

I glared at his door, a matte black rectangle as dark and foreboding as the walls of the metal section he controlled like some fanatic despot over at the Record Huis.

A silver pentagram hung centered on the door. Ominous when seen from across the room, nestled, like me, among floral couch cushions. But it was just aluminum foil wrapped around a piece of cardboard x-actoed into pentagrammatical form. A diabolical pizza box or, really, one of those round mats packaged to protect your frozen pie. A pizza coaster. Euro large by the look of it. Not quite the length of my foot. In America, that's the personal size.

He'd cut the star's points out so the figure was inscribed in a circle. Like he'd used some cheesy pizza wedge as a straight edge. A pentaslice.

14

Goat Song Sacrifice

The room rumbled. A deep thrumming filtered through the closed door. The pentagram shook just the slightest. In an obvious show of commitment to his instrument, Svart had started practicing his bass. The trumpeting of a self-satisfied bullfrog. Svart kept a tiny amp on his nightstand and often played while he sat in bed. I could make out the opening bassline of "Winterminion Ensorcels," the closest thing we had to a new song, even though it used the same riff as the epic title track of Desekration's last release, "To Winds ov Demise." Just stressed on different notes. We'd switched it up, progressed from "To-may-toe" to "To-mah-toe."

I sighed. This new one, "to-mah-toe," sounded stupid. "Winterminion Ensorcels"—the riff and the title. Or at least I thought so. But what did I know? In a new country, a new city, I couldn't play anything right. I couldn't say anything right. I couldn't even say the name of the city right. Gent. It doesn't look hard to say. It's just four letters long. It was like an unpronounceable tetragrammaton that constantly eluded me. I either hocked the word from my throat like a squashy phlegm marble, or I said it without inflection at all, like some guileless tourist, some khakied Rick Steves begirdled with a bulging fanny pack.

You wouldn't think it mattered, but it did. In Dutch, how you say the word depends on where you're from. Even though it's spelled with a "g," people from the city, all the Gentenaars, pronounced it with an "h," like "Hent," but with just the slightest edge. An "h" that cuts like a serrated blade. A dull bread knife sawing through a day old pumpernickel log.

You couldn't get too throaty, though. Like, when Katrin asked me how I did on that first Dutch quiz and I grimaced, drew my finger across my throat, and spat out some sandpapered syllable, something like "chth" or "gkhth." Well, that's the wrong way to say the city's name. You couldn't say "Chthent," or, more obviously, "Ghent," even though that's the English spelling. If you did, you sounded like you came from the Netherlands or, worse, Germany.

I wished they'd given the place a name I could say. Called it "Tomato." At least then, there're only two options. I could have avoided this altogether by calling it Gand, like the French. Some people did that. Like Svart's mom. But Svart convinced me that's not just wrong, it's offensive. You do that, it's like ceding the town to the Walloons, he'd say. He hated them.

It was a nuance I just couldn't get. I had the same problem with my guitar playing. I was technically contracted—bonded by a toothpick-pricked blot of blood on a beer coaster—to produce at least one album for Despondent Abyss, what Svart regarded as the most underground label in existence. Though I was his ticket in, I couldn't shake the feeling I'd fallen back to guitar niveau een.

My guitar and I were foreigners unable to make sounds that had meaning. Its sound, downtuned a half step since I first played in Valhalla, was too guttural, too what Svart called "chunky."

"Downtuned does not equal evil," he'd say, or just "Chunkachunkachunka, when will you learn?"

It was easier to retune, move back to standard, than it was to say "Gent." And it sounded just as bad. My mighty E minor came out flat, nasal. Like one of Paul Simon's roadies had secretly neutered my guitar.

In Svart's room, he flailed his way through the end of the song. The part where, eventually, someone would sing, "Winterminion ensorcels winterminion ensorcels winterminion ensorcels winterminion ensorcels winterminion ensorcels winterminion ensorcels" really fast and, preferably, on a single breath. Good luck. Svart had already rejected a few guys in town who tried out to be our singer. That was the part he used as his nekrobarometer. No one made it through. I saw one guy pull out an inhaler after Svart dismissed him.

Chastened by the memory of that guy stumbling away, sucking down some albuterol, I scooted over to the edge of the couch and pulled my backpack out of my small pile of worldly possessions. It sat sandwiched between the keyboard I'd brought along for the Katabasis tour and a stack of neatly folded laundry. Svart's mom did my laundry. She cooked for us. I once caught her dusting the top edge of his tinfoil pentagram.

I might be at niveau een, I thought, but it's really not so bad. I resolved to play guitar and speak Dutch ... betterly. More better? I'm niveau een at a lot of things.

I figured the best place to start was with my oldest pending assignment. A listening assignment. From Nekrokor. The guy's real name was Bård, Bart of the Norseland, but "Nekrokor" suited him better. Sullen and evil, he made Svart seem like a cookie-stuffed Girl Scout.

I unzipped my backpack and pulled out the CD Nekrokor slipped me after we met. After he signed me to his label. It was by his band, Astrampsychos. Svart's favorite band. Nekrokor told me to study it. I guess that's why I hadn't listened to it. If you had to study something, a point made clear for me in Dutch class, then you hadn't mastered it. You weren't in control.

Like Svart's door, the cover art was a uniform block of black. I hadn't even opened it since moving in with Svart. I last looked at it with Juan, and only then to see if he could help me decode the illegible manifesto, called "On Life and Total Death," spattered in icy blue all caps Old English font across the center of the otherwise completely black, and blank, booklet. It said things like "**TOTAL DEATH IS A SYSTEMATIC PURSUIT OF ENDINGS**" and "**WE SEEK ONLY TOTAL DEATH, AND ONLY TO SPREAD ITS FESTERING GRIP**." It was like the raving gospel of some Anti-Oprah. It didn't say "live your life," but "die your death."

I pried the CD out of the case, walked over to the stereo, and plunked it in. Svart's practice session ended almost as soon as I pushed play. He had a preternatural ability to detect any disturbance of the stereo. Or, really, any disturbance of the copy of "To Winds" he usually kept cued up on the turntable. His door cracked open. I didn't even have the volume that high. And the only sound at that point was a crowd shouting, in the kind of group cheer fashion you hear at Euro football matches, "As-tram-psy-chos," with synchronized clapping thrown in between syllables.

Svart took two Sasquatch steps across the living room and landed next to me on the couch. He grabbed the jewel case and booklet out of my hands.

"I didn't know you had this. It's hard to come by," he said.

"What? *On Life and Total Death*?" I thought that was the name of the album.

"That's not what it's called."

He jumped up and twisted the volume higher.

"This is Astrampsychos. *Live in Brno*."

4.
Salamiblast

"Brno. It's east. A Czech city. They did a show there in an abandoned munitions depot. It had been abandoned since the 1940s. A bunch of squatters took it over. Astrampsychos has done a lot of crazy shows, but this one—I mean, the show, even the recording—this one is legendary. Here. Hand me the case."

I passed it over. Through the speakers, the football chant continued: "As-tram-psy-chos."

"See—even this cover. Amazing, man."

He pointed at it, a color swatch for Sherwin-Williams tone #666, "Eternal Dark."

"This thing's heel limited. Ultralimited, like you say. But in a real way. Not because no one wants it. That thing is rare. Not a lot of copies were made."

I grimaced and leaned back into the couch cushions. I didn't bother defending myself. The last album I made, *In Circle of Ouroboros*, came out on Plutonic Records through what they called their Ultralimited Underground series. At the time, I stupidly took this to mean that they saw the music as a groundbreaking release that underground metal fans worldwide would recognize as a bold expansion of the genre's sonic range. I mean, that's pretty much what the label guys wrote in their ad copy for the thing. It took me awhile to realize they'd invented the series as a way to wash their hands of me. Release an ultralimited number of discs, send me on tour to sell them, then move on to something new, some fresh set of clueless clods with enough of a hometown following to drum up some sales.

Besides, Svart was brutally honest about everything. And not just to me. His mom kissed him on the cheek one evening when she got home from work. We were sitting on the couch, drinking beers before going out to drink some more. She leaned over me to do it. He frowned, then said, "Mom, I can totally see your tits. I bet David can, too." And he was right.

Plus, it didn't hurt that I'd turned "ultralimited" into a catch all expression, my own little scrap of imported American slang. After a night of drinking, when Svart would throw open the drapes and say, in a loud, chipper voice, "Goeie morgen, David! How do you feel?" I'd groan, pull the sheet over my face, and croak, "ultralimited." Or, when he tried to teach me some Desekration riff and I flubbed it, I'd stop playing before he had a chance to berate me and say something like "Let me try again. That one was ultralimited."

Svart saw his crushing frankness as a European virtue. If I told him it wasn't necessary to point out all the limitations of my ultralimited release, he'd just say something like, "We say what we mean. We're direct. You Americans, you talk more, but you never say what you mean. You don't know what you mean."

So, I didn't respond. Instead, I considered what kind of sandwich I'd make for myself later. I hadn't had anything since lunch, and I knew there was some salami—the kind you can't get in America, that U.S. Customs tries to confiscate unless you hide it in a pair of dirty socks or something—in the refrigerator.

Svart went on, cradling the case in his palms: "The only thing harder to find than this one is the very first pressing. On vinyl."

On the stereo, the music started in earnest. Fast. Loud. Poorly recorded. I didn't get why Svart had such a hard-on for these guys. If anything, the singer sounded a bit more strangulated than usual. Like a gremlin howling through the firm dual chokeholds of autoerotic asphyxiation.

"You know how you can tell if you have the first pressing?"

I didn't.

"You see how this whole cover is black? Well, they fucked up at the printer on the first pressing. It's pink. Just a big patch of pink. Like a fag flag or something. Ha!"

"I bet Nekrokor loved that." Sherwin-Williams tone #66, "Delicate Manties."

"No joke! You know what happened to the printer?" He leaned forward, resting one of his elephantine elbows on the coffee table. "He died. Just a few weeks after he fixed the problem, too. I heard that one of these guys—I don't know which one—they laid a curse on him."

"A curse?"

"Yeah—I know it sounds crazy. But that's what happened. The cops could never prove anything, but the guy just went," he furrowed his brow, "like, into a coma or something. Then, his heart stopped."

"Here." He skipped ahead a few tracks. "This is the part you need to hear."

I heard a pop, followed by a loud thump, like someone dropped the microphone.

"That was a grenade."

"A grenade?"

"Like I said, it was in an old munitions factory. Someone found it, climbed to the roof, and threw it off the building."

"Did anyone die?"

"No. Not from the grenade. A few people came close, though."

A scratchy croak of a voice came on after the pop, and said, "King Death claims another victim. All hail the king ... the king of Hell."

"That's Nordikron, the singer," Svart said.

Then, you hear a muffled shuffling. It sounded like a dog sniffing the mic head.

Or someone trying to breathe through a mask. Svart filled me in. The whole time they were playing, the band shared the stage with a mock crucifixion scene. Three dudes, naked except for hoods on their heads, tied to crosses on stage. Apparently, the grenade shook the building enough so that one of the crosses, and the guy on it, fell onto the stage. The singer held the microphone up to the guy, who had just about fainted, but left the mask on the guy's head.

After some more mic snuffling, Nordikron's voice came on again, "He expresses it better than I can, this servant, what the next song is about," followed by a raptor shriek, barely decipherable as the song title, "Serviam Sathanas."

"Holy shit! Was the guy okay?" I asked.

Svart seemed bemused.

"Of course. All of them were. They did this willingly. They got paid. Something like $25 each. Clearly, they got ripped off, but it serves them right. They had to have known what they were getting into. These songs are still the old stuff. The new one is much advanced."

He disappeared into his room to get the new Astrampsychos album, *The Intrapsychic Secret*.

Goat Song Sacrifice

I shifted over to the stereo and turned the volume down. As low as it could go without turning it off. Svart wouldn't like that at all, but what he'd told me, what I'd heard, unsettled me. I mean, I was no innocent, no David Seville harmonizing "Jingle Bells" through helium tokes. I played death metal. I made an album called *Thrones of Satanic Dominion*. But this went too far. You can't kill your fans, or the people helping you put on your show. Our music sounded scary, too, but at the end of the day, we thought we were the good guys. Good because we weren't afraid to reflect the badness of what we saw around us. A song about nuclear annihilation could be a cry for peace. A grunt for peace. At a Valhalla show, Phil always insisted on sticking around to hand out guitar picks and talk to any kids who hung around after our set. And the Bard, well, he just wanted to love some plus-size women.

But this guy, Nordikron, as he wailed and choked out the words "Serviam Sathanas," I think he meant it. He really wanted to serve Satan. And, whatever he thought that meant, it clearly didn't involve passing out guitar picks and glad handing with the kids.

Svart emerged from his room holding the gatefold vinyl version of the follow up to *Live in Brno*. They called it *The Intrapsychic Secret*. A bit more thought went into the cover design of this one. First, it actually had a cover design. It featured a huge white circle that, from across the room, looked like the moon.

Svart came back to the couch and handed the record over to me. Up close, you could see that it was a map, a cosmic diagram of the universe taken from a medieval manuscript, showing the earth surrounded by a series of interlocking spheres and arcane symbols. A series of Latin words, "Coelum Empireum Habitaculum Dei et Omnium Electorum," circled the outermost sphere. It means "The Empire of Heaven, Home of God and All the Elect." A thin red line in the shape of a pentagram had been carefully inscribed across the face of the diagram. The pentagram clarified which "Dei" the band's elect listeners should venerate. It didn't deface the ancient image of an earth-centered cosmos. It complemented, it Satanized, medieval reality.

Goat Song Sacrifice

The band logo and album title framing the top and bottom of the cosmic map were relatively restrained. The only nod to the prevailing fashion of ornate, symmetrical lettering laden with occult symbols was the profusion of branches emanating from the edges of each letter.

They weren't quite as stiff or rectilinear as branches, really. They were more like the curving tendrils of roots, the dense rhizomatic clusters channeling beneath the earth.

Some of the roots from the "A" and "S" in "Astrampsychos" snaked down and knotted into the sketchy lettering of the title at the bottom of the cover.

This wasn't the first time I'd seen *The Intrapsychic Secret.* Svart showed it to me the day I met him. I still have no idea what it means, though. The title. Svart said it had something to do with the psychic pain inflicted on the living by the spirits of all the people who died in the plague. You know, the Black Plague. The one that happened six hundred years ago. Somehow, we're still afflicted by the trauma of their deaths. Or something like that. Svart and I talked about this a few times and he always got irate when I asked the obvious follow up question—"So, these guys believe in ghosts?"

"It's so crazy that you met Nekrokor. That he signed you. That he thinks you can make something good enough for Despondent Abyss," Svart said as he sat back down. The indoctrination process went both ways. I forced him to listen to my stuff. I gave Svart a copy of *In Circle of Ouroboros* when I moved in. He was not a fan.

I handed out copies of that thing to everyone I knew. My Dutch teacher. Svart's mom. Katrin. Anything to get that stack out of my backpack. Lighten my load. Besides, I figured, it's not like anyone's going to buy them.

"It's lucky for you that you met me." This was another point Svart made on a regular basis. "For real. You don't wanna fuck with that guy. Any of those guys. That Katabasis thing—that's not gonna cut it. Sounds like a vacuum cleaner."

He hummed, imitating one of my moody, introspective riffs.

"Every once in a while, it picks up some bits of cereal."

He chattered, imitating one of Juan's atonal, meandering solos.

"And how can I forget . . ." he gestured to the keyboard I brought on tour, now discarded like a child's toy in the far corner.

"Klote. Have you told him yet, Nekrokor, that we have joined forces? I'm sure he knows Desekration. I'm certain of it."

He knew this because he sent an unsolicited copy of "To Winds ov Demise" to the PO Box address listed on the back cover of every Despondent Abyss release. He brought this up at least once a day, usually when he came in with the mail, his face gray, set in stone, as he dumped his mom's bills and bank statements on the kitchen table. Nekrokor had yet to reply. He hadn't even taken the time to pen a personalized death threat, the envelope garnished with toxic sludge, like he had for me. He hadn't taken the time to show he cared.

And every day, Svart would ask me again about the initial

death threat letter I received when I lived in Miami. The timeline. How long had the first Valhalla album been out? Was I absolutely sure I hadn't tried to reach him first?

Svart, always forthright and direct, didn't understand this. Svart, so compulsive and persistent, couldn't let it go. Besides, he'd say while rooting through his mom's mail, just to make sure he hadn't overlooked some slim reply, some grim postcard, he'd even dutifully stuffed the package he mailed to Nekrokor with International Reply Coupons. More than are required, he'd say.

Sure, Nekrokor might curse people. He may have threatened me with a knife. And his bandmates seemed to think nothing of asphyxiating their human props in the midst of a performance. But engage in mail fraud?

Unbelooflijk.

Unbelievable, Svart would say when I brought up the possibility that his postage—about five bucks worth—may have been used elsewhere. May have been affixed to a lovingly crafted death threat in transit to some down on their luck death metal band in Luxembourg. Or Tasmania, even, with all those IRCs Svart sent.

If I'd brought Nekrokor's death threat letter along, packed it in my carry-on, I could have easily sold it to Svart. Unfortunately, it was moldering in my sister's spare bedroom. The soon to be baby's room. I hoped the green sludge caked in the envelope's creases wasn't noxious. Wouldn't befoul the nursery air. Though Nekrokor would celebrate that kind of thing, no doubt. If I hear she's pregnant, I told myself, I'll call her. Tell her or, better, her husband, to go through my stuff and throw the thing away.

"Ha. You are so lucky," Svart said. "If I had that letter, I'd frame it. I'd hang it right here."

He pointed to the wall above the couch, where there was

some kind of tapestry with a Belgian landscape, a wide field flanked by canals and dotted with windmills.

"I didn't feel lucky when I got it. Or when I met him in person. Him and his knife."

"I know. I can't believe it. It was this knife, wasn't it?"

He flipped the cover over and pointed at Nekrokor's photo on the back. There was one of each member, their faces smeared with corpsepaint. This was when it was still rare—something new and forbidding. Before you could play Guitar Hero as a lovable nekrolummox. Even then, someone in that group understood they were presenting themselves not as real people, but as characters designed to tap into the escapist fantasies of their fans. They'd even shaped the inky streaks on their faces into different patterns: on one, they looked like the dual wings of some floating menace, some vampiric butterfly; on another, a sharp triangle colored around each eye made me think of a radioactivity hazard sign. Nekrokor, who, in my brief dealings with him hadn't appeared overly concerned with personal maintenance, took the minimalist route. It seemed like he'd raised the horns, dipped his index finger and pinky into the ink pot, then drawn them down his face, down his neck, even, from his eyelids to his Adam's apple, probably before wiping whatever was left on his pants. The round black wells circling each of Nordikron's eyes emphasized the orbits of the skull beneath the skin.

I'd seen these pictures before, instantly recognized Nekrokor and his knife the first time Svart showed me *The Intrapsychic Secret*. Instantly recognized the name of my group, Katabasis, in the list of forthcoming Despondent Abyss releases below the song titles.

The borders of the pictures were encased in a series of drawn frames that looked like the columns and gabled roofs of a series of Roman temples. Each one had a different symbol centered where, if they were really temples, you'd have some chiseled frieze of gods streaming past in chariots. One had a pentagram, another had an inverted cross, and the third one had a hammer or something. The last one, a circle with eight arrow points, looked like a Ninja Turtle's shuriken.

Really, these guys were like Ninja Turtles, or some other superhero troupe, each with his symbol, his weapon, his special musical power, and his name splayed out in Satanic calligraphy underneath. Nekrokor, as I've told you, had his knife, a nasty-looking blade with a rounded pommel studded with nails. He stood, shirtless, with crossed arms, and seemed to be staring directly over the shoulder of whoever took the picture. He got the pentagram.

Underneath the inverted cross, Nordikron wielded a long

root that snaked wildly around the frame, clumps of dirt splattering everywhere. He pointed toward the heavens, his mouth wide open in what looked like maniacal laughter. In a bold, for metal, sartorial move, he wore a tight white t-shirt. Its stretched out neck revealed his slender collar bones; the whole thing was covered in mud splotches and black-ringed holes burned into the fabric.

"Who's this guy?" I asked, pointing at a dude wearing a colander or something on his head. A metal helmet, its round sides rising to a point. He had on sleeveless chainmail, like a medieval muscle shirt, over a black long sleeved shirt. Unlike Nekrokor and Nordikron, he looked peaceful, eyes upturned, his arms crossed over his chest, both hands clasped in the sign of the horns. You could see he was in a forest, flanked by evergreens.

"Oh, that's Torburn. The drummer. You know, he used to be on the Olympic cycling team."

"He was in the Olympics?"

"Well . . . he qualified. But, drug tests."

He mimicked hitting a joint.

"Weed. They were looking for steroids or something, he was so fast. But they got him for weed."

He described Torburn's regimen, how he approached drumming like a sport.

"Or at least that's how he used to do it. He's slipping lately. Too many brownies. He needs to take some steroids. To get him back on track. Plus, those side projects."

He groaned.

"Have you ever heard of Hamertijd? Folk music. He plays a tambourine. There's a flute player, too. It's not metal."

"Hammertime?" I asked.

Too legit.

"Yes, something like that. It means the time of the hammer. He thinks he's a Viking. A stoner Viking. God." He pinched the bridge of his nose and sighed, like he was smoking weed. Exhaling a stinky smoke cloud. "I hope I never do something like that."

My stomach grumbled. Really, he'd just expelled a blast of salami-infused air toward me. A salamiblast. I felt like I had the munchies, my hunger stoked by the smell of whatever greasy pork chunks remained wedged in Svart's gumline.

I tried to get up, head to the refrigerator to make that sandwich before it was too late. Had he already eaten it all?

"Hohoh! And this one, A. Hex. What a beast."

He put his hand on my knee and pushed me back into the couch cushions.

The last guy held an axe in one hand; his other hand gripped the air like he suffered some rare form of palsy. I pointed at the symbol, the ninja star.

"What's that?" I asked.

"That's the sign of chaos. It suits him. He works as a security guard, like at a minimum security prison, but I heard that he got arrested for assault recently. Now he's a guard, but soon, he'll be a prisoner. And on the bass? He breaks strings all the time. You ever play the bass? Those strings are thick. You can hear it, too."

"Hey, wait a second. Let me see that!"

I grabbed the cover from Svart and studied it closely.

"He's wearing a Valhalla shirt!"

He had on a shirt they made for our song "Zombichrist." It had a green skinned Jesus munching on a severed hand.

"Hmm. I'd never noticed that," Svart said, deflated. He didn't like Katabasis, but he wouldn't even listen to Valhalla, my first band. He considered *Thrones of Satanic Dominion* to be pop music as cloying and plastic as Mariah Carey's latest endeavor.

"Maybe he wore it as a joke? Oh, wait. Here it is." He held up his finger and nodded his head along with the high speed tumult.

After a few seconds, a loud twang jolted through the speakers. It didn't sound so different from the pop of the grenade he'd played for me earlier. Someone said "shit" in a normal speaking voice. It wasn't Nordikron. The rest of the group flailed on, but it suddenly sounded like they were transmitted through a cheap clock radio.

"Ha ha!" Svart clapped. "The bass. You hear that? It's the most important piece." He went on for a few minutes, reminding me about the important position of the bass, about how my job was to complement his playing, and not the other way around.

"Uh huh," I nodded. No use disputing Svart's lo-end theory.

"Now let's hear the real masterwork."

He ambled over to the stereo and switched off *Live in Brno* in the midst of some intersong groaning. Whether it was Nordikron or one of his mock-crucified backup singers, I

33

still couldn't tell.

"They stole my riff," he beamed and dropped the needle onto *The Intrapsychic Secret*.

5.
The Miseducation of David Fosberg

Svart was right. Not the part about the riff—that was bullshit. He thought a pretty standard note progression on the song "Four Temples" confirmed, in his words, they "felt the assault" of the flimsy 7" he sent to them. But if that was true, then most songs made up of notes have been equally blasphemated by his diabolicrusade.

He was right that *The Intrapsychic Secret* deserved—deserves—to be called a masterwork. I'm sure you know that. Who doesn't regale it as the musical highlight of that period? Even today, when I click through some tedious listicle of the top ten metal albums ever, there it is, a little JPEG of the medieval engraving of the Ptolemaic system gracing its cover, followed by a caption about the events that happened after its release. The really astute music writers even throw in a reference to Desekration, point out our involvement in the whole thing.

It's the record that a hundred other bands copied. The one that got another hundred, every other band that sounded like Valhalla, or had a Dan Seagrave cover, or recorded at Morrisound, booted from their labels. It's the one that gave black metal a separate identity, an identity based as much on ideas and worldview, or Weltanschauung if you're really cult, as on the actual sound. It's the one that made it something like a religion, a creed, a coven of heresiarchs obsessed with macrocosmological arcana.

Maybe I'm just biased. I mean, Astrampsychos wasn't the first black metal band. So many of them popped up at that time, and in different places. Greece, South America, even a few emerged from the ashes of the American death metal scene. And, I'm sure you're thinking this, I'm leaving out the biggest enclave of corpsepainted lunacy, the guys from Oslo and Bergen who got all the press. I know that story, too. I read *Lords of Chaos*. Really, I read about it through monthly installments in *Terrorizer* as Norway's diabolic summer blazed. And I'm pretty certain that somewhere along the line, Nekrokor spent at least a bit of time holding court in Helvete's storied basement. He had to. Who else was buying, and maybe even selling, Despondent Abyss releases in those early days?

But I wasn't there. You only get the story I know. Besides, those same web captions make a similar point. The thing about what happened in Belgium the year that I lived there was that it pointedly wasn't stoked into hysteria by dramatic headlines and courtroom hijinks. I mean, it's Belgium. Even its version of black metal animus was understated and subtle. No one even knew what happened, or even cared, until much later. When they found the body.

The reason people still talk about Astrampsychos, about *The Intrapsychic Secret*, about the follow up that never was, is that the tragedy could have happened anywhere. Anyone could have been ensnared. Anyone, including me.

And as soon as I heard it, I knew that, for once, Svart was using the word "masterwork" in the right way. Well, not as soon as I heard it. But pretty close. About ten seconds in, it gripped me and wouldn't let go. It still hasn't let go. Despite everything that happened, I still break out *The Intrapsychic Secret* at least once a week. At first, you just hear static. You think you're in for another lo-fi letdown. That first time I heard it, Svart bumped up the volume just as the static resolved into the sound of wind. Or at least the cycling whoosh of wind as imagined by Casio's sound engineers. I considered asking Svart why these guys could use a keyboard while mine was the source of so much scorn, but at that moment, Nordikron's overpowering shriek, no synthesized effect but a force like the life devouring breath of Boreas, filled the room. No lie, I felt the room grow about five degrees colder.

Then, a slow riff from a single guitar, Nekrokor's guitar, emerged through the jagged hole cut by Nordikron's voice and churned through a brief sequence of high pitched notes. You could picture Nekrokor, clad in some ancient muscle-t, shoulders caked with dandruff, standing on the summit of a Nordic peak, one foot propped on a craggy spur as though it were an amp resonating with the power of his mighty riffing. And Nordikron, next to him, screaming the rest of the world into existence.

Amazingly, you could decipher the lyrics, too. He didn't just scream; he screamed intelligibly. Like some hyperliterate cacodaemon summoned to read to the blind. Plus, the gatefold included all the lyrics, and printed them in a font that didn't require a cryptanalyst's decoding expertise.

But that's not reason alone to celebrate it. Prior to that, I counted intelligibility as a black mark, in a bad way, against a singer. I didn't want to know the lyrics, and preferred to listen to them as another form of percussion. If the guy couldn't evoke a burbling plumbing disaster through the power of his throat, I didn't want to hear it. Nordikron didn't just open my ears to the many pleasures of the abraded tonsil approach common in black metal; he also made me feel like I had discovered something totally new and amazing, what metalheads call, unironically, "clean" singing. What everyone else just calls singing. My parents would thank him if they could.

Midway through that first song, "The Inmost Sanctum," it was like the band collectively realized they had transcended the need to conform to any of metal's generic features. That the riff forming the beginning of the song is so self-evidently majestic and powerful as to comprise the first hymn in some codex celebrating the arrival of a new dark age. That they had no need to maintain the artificial trappings of modern music, of electric instruments, of stylized vocalizings.

If the first half of the song sounded like the members of Astrampsychos should be invoking the majestic throne of Satan from the highest peak they could access with a four track and an extension cord, the second part made me think the band had adjourned to some small cave, or hut, some Neolithic sanctuary, to shelter them from the wind swirling around the peak. The plucking of an acoustic guitar masquerading as a lute broke through the dying whine of a sustained one-note solo. A campfire—not some studio effect, but a real fire if I'm not mistaken—crackled in the background. Then, Nekrokor and Nordikron engaged in what I could only call a duet, if that word didn't suggest some hot and heavy R&B couple lubing up for the quiet storm. Nekrokor asked a series of questions in a kind of sung speaking and Nordikron answered in the strong and resonant voice of a Wagnerian Heldentenor:

Nekrokor: Where have you come from?
Nordikron: From the world of the first chosen.
Nekrokor: Whither do you want to go?

Goat Song Sacrifice

Nordikron: To the inmost sanctum.
Nekrokor: What do you seek?
Nordikron: He who is, and was, and always shall be.
Nekrokor: What inspires you?
Nordikron: The fire, which lives in me and is now
           ablaze.

This interlude didn't last long, though. As soon as Nordikron sang the word "ablaze," all the modern elements came streaming back in. Like the mountain tempest blew in and stoked the fire into a consuming inferno. Nordikron hyperventilated through that last line, "The fire, which lives in me and is now ablaze," a few times, then truncated it into a song-ending, testicle-squashing crescendo of "the fire is now ablaze," leaving me and Svart staring at each other grinning as the hissing of the fire slowly faded away.

"That's amazing," I said.

Svart nodded.

We listened to the rest of the album in silence. It was like the misshapen mess of *Live in Brno*, the dischronic discordance of the first Bathory albums, the random grunts of Tom G. Warrior, had all been rearranged and reassembled into their ideal form. Everything had a place and a reason. In another song, they had even found a way to extract the full emotional impact of A. Hex and his brutal, string-snapping bass technique. The string breaks with a loud thump, just like on *Live in Brno*. Then, the rest of the song continues, but with a sound as tinny and frail as if it streamed through a rusted gramophone horn. The volume slowly increases until an explosion rocks through the speakers and the bass emerges back into the mix.

When *The Intrapsychic Secret* ended, I needed to hear it again. It was one of those albums that made you feel like you had no choice but to listen to it repeatedly. It enthralled in the true sense of the word—it made you its thrall.

It was so good, I even forgot I wanted a sandwich.

6.
A Slaapkamer of One's Own

You know how, when someone's not getting something done, people say they're dicking around? They're jerking off? Well, a few weeks after Svart converted me to the sublime pleasures of Astrampsychos, my pursuit of other, less sublime pleasures resulted in my escape from the couch. Svart's mom helped me escape the couch. Not long after she interrupted a solitary ritual of self-flagellation. She could tell I needed some alone time. Some me time. Maybe it was more expulsion than escape.

One afternoon, she walked in just as I'd lathered up with a dollop of Nivea I'd found in the medicine chest. Svart wasn't home. As soon as I heard the metallic clink of the key in the lock, I moved fast. I scooped up the wad of toilet paper I'd positioned next to the bottle of skin moisturizer on the coffee table. I smeared the goo from all offending appendages, even getting the globs pooled in the crevices between my fingers. I stuffed myself back into my pants, wiped any lingering cream on my pant legs, and tossed the sodden wad of toilet paper to the ground. I stepped on it, then scanned the front page of *De Gentenaar*, the local newspaper, straining to make out any words I might actually know. Straining to will my boner away.

A second later, she stood in the kitchen to find me, a model of right living and the picture of an ideal houseguest, reading the paper in a clear effort at self-betterment.

"Chapped skin, eh?" she said as soon as she set her purse and a tote bag full of her students' homework on the kitchen counter.

I blanched. She knew, but how? I thought she could smell my guilt, or somehow detect the faintest trace of creamy peach hanging in the air. I set the paper down, carefully laying it across my lap. That's when I realized I hadn't put the bottle away. It stood on the coffee table, next to the other sections of the paper.

I tried to play it off. What else could I do?

"Yeah. This air," I said. "It's a lot drier than home. And colder than I'm used to."

She smirked, then disappeared into her room.

It's true I should have been stealthier. More cautious. Maybe taken a long shower instead. Not even Svart would burst in there. He regularly disappeared into the bathroom for massive, hour-long feats of defecation. He'd suspect nothing. But there wasn't really a shower. Just a curtainless tub with a showerhead at the end of a plastic hose. A Eurospritz. I mean, I tried it once, late at night, when Svart's mom was asleep and he'd glued himself to some Belgian gameshow. Water sprayed the floor, even the ceiling, before I gave up. I can't man two nozzles at once.

Maybe on some level I wanted her to catch me? She's not unattractive, though she somehow squeezed Svart, colossal skull and all, out into the world. Even the older Euroladies stay fit and trim. They accessorize with orange silk scarves that cover the neck, but not the cleavage. She wore this dark plum lipstick that you could smell long after she left the apartment. Maybe somewhere, in the deepest reptilian crevices of my mind, I imagined she'd walk in right at the apex of a greasy pull. That she'd still say something clever, like "Chapped skin, eh?" but then she'd strip down and exfoliate my dick with her purple lips.

A rookie move, for sure. I should have known better. She usually got home not long after I did. Her classes ended at the same time as mine. It's just—those couple of hours were the only Svartless time I had. Besides, I was provoked. I came out of school that day to find a row of yogurt posters plastered across the wall on the other side of the street. Five or six posters stretched to the top of the wall. Usually, it was collaged with a jumble of club flyers, rental notices, and movie posters in various stages of decay. That's right—yogurt posters. For the kind that you drink. Drinkyoghurt.

It's not like I had some kind of dairy fetish, despite its creamy consistency. Each poster had a life size image of a topless girl emerging from a pristine swimming pool. The azure Mediterranean in the background. She wore a white bikini bottom, the couture kind with a golden buckle. She had her hair slicked behind her ears and a photo enhanced spray of water droplets artfully spattered across her neck, her throat, her breasts.

Her breasts. They were as brown and shiny as egg glazed dinner rolls. She might as well have been swimming in baby oil. A row of sun-bronzed areolae stretched across the wall. To make matters worse, she held a white bottle of this drinkyoghurt stuff in one of her hands. She held it above her head. Above her mouth. She squeezed out the last drop, like the bottle was some albino dong streaming from the heavens. A milky dot of drinkyoghurt, perfect and round, sat centered on the tip of her pink outstretched tongue.

It was too much for me. It had been too long. I felt my own drinkyoghurt curdling deep within. I hurried home. I limped past the Record Huis and down the hill like a champion of the three-legged race.

A few days after that, I woke up with a folded newspaper across my face. I opened it to find a list of rental ads—a line of short descriptions all titled "Te Huur." Svart's mom sat at the kitchen table sipping a cup of coffee.

Through the kitchen window, rain fell, cold and insistent. More and more the days started this way, in a gray haze the sun seemed powerless to burn through. The trees still had leaves, but it seemed unlikely any photosynthesizing was going down. Vestigial leaves. Soon, they would fall. The temperature, too. From my tropical mindset, these signs seemed both unsettling and unreal. I'd never endured a real winter. Or thought of it bringing anything more unpleasant than a deluge of French Canadian tourists.

"The air's not dry today, is it?" she said.

She'd taken the trouble to highlight some of the ads for me, but I couldn't make sense of real estate abbreviations in English, let alone Dutch. I barely knew the word for bedroom, slaapkamer. How would you abbreviate it? Slp? Spk? Skm? Plus, the ads listed apartment sizes in square meters. No help at all to my metrically challenged mind. How many square meters did a single guy need? I had no idea. Translating rents into dollars pushed my cognitive limits.

I sat at the table and asked her to help.

"Can you go with me to see some of these?"

She peered at me over the edge of her cup and smiled.

"I thought you'd never ask. You need your own space! And poor Jurgen," she glanced over at Svart's closed door.

"He means well, but he's not always the easiest on his friends. I will meet you after school—right outside the front door."

She stood up and put her empty coffee cup on the table. A purple lipstick crescent stained the brim. Then, she picked up a stack of graded exams.

"Now, let's go. Your class starts at nine, just like mine, and I know that Helena doesn't appreciate tardiness."

Later that afternoon, Mrs. Svart and I stepped out of the rental office on the ground floor of my new home, a studio in a slate gray building on a street of tightly compacted apartment blocks adjacent to a large city park. A wide sidewalk ran along Rooseveltlaan, a relatively busy road that zoomed out to the intercity highway a mile or so away. I mean, it wasn't as traffic choked as anything comparable at home, but I'd started to adjust to the smaller scale of Belgian life. When I first moved in with Svart, I thought most of the streets in his neighborhood looked more like bike paths.

I couldn't have done it without her. And not just because of the language, the documents, the impenetrable legalese rendered in impenetrable Dutch. Renting a Belgian apartment for a few months required more paperwork than buying, registering, and insuring a car in the states. And earlier that afternoon, I didn't even think we'd ever find a place to rent. One apartment, right above a Chinese restaurant, reeked of cooking oil. The walls had a filmy brown sheen from the omnipresent fog of boiled fat. They might as well have just wallpapered the place with fried wonton wrappers. Another one reminded me of Raskolnikov's grim garret, the kind of place you wanted pre-equipped with a gas oven, a sturdy hook in the ceiling, and a very short lease. One window, the size of this book, faced out of a gauzy pane of fogged plexiglass to a cracked brick wall.

By the time we made it to the Rooseveltlaan building, I worried I wouldn't find anything better than the Svartian couch. With or without its suspicious stains. But as soon as we stepped through the marbled doorway and encountered the rental agent, a clean cut guy holding a clipboard, I started to worry about something else. I went from thinking "there's no way I can live in this stinky shithole" or "there's no way I can live in this depressing shithole" to "there's no way they'll let this stinky shitbag—me—live here."

The agent wore a close fitting navy suit with a paisley tie and pearl cufflinks. Shiny brown loafers. His hair, slightly frosted with gray, lay as clean and orderly as a newly tilled field. You could tell he owned a comb.

He introduced himself, shook our hands, then took us up to see the place. I didn't say anything. Occasionally, he'd make some comment toward me and I'd smile, nod, mutter "ja" in my best niveau een voice.

I liked the place. Small, but clean. Furnished. No discernible odor. You entered through a small kitchen and into a single room. One slaapkamer. A wall-length unit of blond wood cabinets stood on the left side of the kamer. I'd do my slaaping on the right side, where a futon lay on a shin-high frame. A small, white tiled bathroom adjoined the main room by the bed. The best feature had to be the glass door and row of windows that led to a small terrace, a terrasje, overlooking a courtyard five floors down. From the terrace, you could see the crumbling grandeur of an old abbey in the distance. And at that height, the afternoon sun streamed through the glass. It warmed the room. This place, I determined, had the advantage of staving off the inevitable ravages of Seasonal Affective Disorder, which, even though it was only August, I'd already begun to dread.

From an American perspective, the room itself amounted

to little more than a glorified dorm, but after some time in Belgium, I knew that the place qualified as "luxe." The view alone counted as a considerable improvement over the view of Coral Gables city hall that I used to think was so great. And any view far surpassed the scenic vista of Svart's bedroom door. Plus, the rent cost about half as much as I'd been paying in Florida.

I don't think the rental agent realized I wasn't Mrs. Svart's son until we went back downstairs into his office and I gave him the completed rental application. He chirped away happily as he sorted through the papers arranged behind his desk. I sat in one of the plush leather chairs facing his desk and scratched all my vital information onto the rental application. When I finished, I leaned back, dug my passport out of my front pocket, then slid the application and passport across the desk.

He stroked his chin, flipped through my passport, then let out a nervous chuckle.

"Mevrouw Svart," he began, revealing a row of teeth as white as piano keys. I can't give you the exact blow by blow of what happened next. That's some niveau twintig material, or higher. At one point, he said "Fosberg," pointed at me, then said "Svart," pointing at her. She clucked something back, readjusted her neck scarf for maximum cleavage display, then said something that sounded like "Yes, he's my son's friend." After that, they chattered back and forth. Clearly, he wasn't thrilled about renting to me, a young guy, a foreigner, of slender means. Occasionally, he looked over at me, to the hair falling across my shoulders. To the flecks of dandruff there, too. A whole galaxy of tiny stars. It didn't help that the nicest shirt I could find was a Katabasis shirt I'd cut the tag out of and worn inside out. My other shirts, all three of them, had faded over time to a kind of dishwater gray. The Katabasis shirt, I'd figured that morning as I hunted through the kitchen for a pair of scissors, had the advantage of full coloration. I'd even fished out the last size medium, thinking that form fitting equals fashion forward.

The agent asked Svart's mom, more than once, if she'd vouch for me. He made her fill out a rental application as well. Before we got out of there, I saw her pull her bank card out of her purse and transcribe the account number onto the form. When he wrote down the number of what I owed before I could move in, I pulled a thick envelope out of my other front pocket and counted out a stack of bills. I paid for the first month's rent, the last month's rent, a security deposit, and a couple hundred dollars of additional fees that, I think, amounted to an asshole tax for my scruffy appearance. The shitbag surcharge. He took the money, but before he signed to finalize everything, he called Mrs. Svart's bank and talked to them for a while. During that time, I resolved to buy at least one shirt with a collar.

As we walked down the Rooseveltlaan to a grocery store on a shopping area called the Rooseveltplein, I soaked in the fact that I was an official property renter in a foreign country. A huurder in a strange land. I worried about the much lighter money envelope in my pocket, but I figured with a lease, I'd be less inclined to fly home, recalibrate the expired date on my return ticket, and otherwise fade away.

Mrs. Svart put her arm around my shoulders, squeezed me, and said, "I'm so happy for you! You're doing the right thing! I lived abroad when I was your age—in Italy—and I still remember that year as the best of my life. Hopefully, some of your adventurousness will rub off on Jurgen. He has no interest in travel. Too single minded, sometimes, like his father."

I nodded. My mom had never hugged me while telling me

I'd done the right thing. If she were my mom, I wouldn't want to leave either.

I did my best to reassure her that I was good for my money. That the Rooseveltlaan agent wouldn't find some reason to siphon out her bank account.

She smiled, tousled my hair, then said, "I'm picking up a few things for dinner. I'll see you back at home." She headed into the grocery store, and I walked across the plaza toward Svart's record shop. I thought I'd see if he was off so we could head home together. Break the news to him.

7.
Curried Remains

I headed across the Rooseveltplein, a large, flat plaza laid with herringboned gray bricks. The grocery store sat at the basement level of an indoor shopping center. I guess you'd call it a mall, but less sprawly. The stores were arranged vertically, not horizontally. Besides the grocery store, there were three or four additional levels for your shopping enjoyment. A Euromall.

I crossed a bridge over a canal that you could see from the terrace of my new apartment. My sanctum sanctorum, removed from Svart's couch and its constant surveillance. My private sanctum was waterfront property. I guess everything's waterfront in this canal crossed city, I thought, running my hand along the curved, rusted guardrail. And by canal, I really mean something like a stream. Scenic and tranquil. Not a dredged trench layered with a goopy smoothie equal parts duck doo and motor oil. Not a Miami-style canal. To my right, a row of porthole windows along the outer wall of the grocery store peered out at the canal. Inside, shoppers squeezed tomatoes and hefted heads of lettuce. In the months to come, I'd do the majority of my living in this area.

Goat Song Sacrifice

Every day, I'd walk the path down Rooseveltlaan, across the plaza, over the bridge, then up the hill to the Record Huis. Sometimes I'd stop at the Vooruit for a coffee. The street had a drug store, a few restaurants—tapas, kebabs, Indian—and a nachtwinkel, a nightstore. It's like a Belgian 7-11 for your late night beer needs.

I ducked into the nachtwinkel to pick up a couple blikjes of Jupiler. I figured that way, Svart would be less bummed when I told him I was abandoning his couch. He was ornery, abusive even, but Mrs. Svart was right: he just wanted to be liked. Inside, I took the two cans and plopped them on the counter. The clerk mumbled the price and stuffed the cans in a plastic bag. I tried out my own Flemish mumble, saying "dank u wel" as I took my beer sack and stepped back out onto the street.

Before I even made it past the tapas place next door, I heard someone call my name. It was a woman's voice. I looked back to the Rooseveltplein, thinking it was Mrs. Svart. I heard my name again, and looked up just in time to see Delphine standing directly in front of me.

I stopped, suspicious. I held up my beers between us, like little aluminum shields. I imagined the Bard poised to pop out from behind or, more likely, underneath the billowing folds of her ankle-length dress. It was made from bluish, nearly purple velvet. Thick cuffs of black lace, ornate and filigreed, cloaked her hands and throat. The velvet gripped her many curves like the fuzzy skin engirdling a peach's ripe fullness. She could have been one of the Fruits of the Loom. A strange fruit. A plum or something, but topped with fringed bangs.

"David . . . so good to see you!"

"Hey, Delphine. You too. Yeah, great."

I started walking. She came with me.

51

"Juan misses you. A lot."

I didn't expect that. He'd looked so happy when I saw them tooling down Overpoortstraat on their bikes. I stopped.

"Really?"

"Yes. He feels bad. You're his friend."

We moved to the edge of the sidewalk and talked. I told her about Dutch class, my new apartment, the new band.

"Yeah, I'm playing with this guy Jurgen—he calls himself Svart. It's pretty cool."

"He works at the Record Huis, the record shop there, on the corner?" she asked.

"Yeah, that's the guy. Big, kind of mean looking. Has a blond afro."

"I've met him before."

I enjoyed hearing that Juan missed me. To make it clear that I did not miss, or need, him, I told Delphine about all my recent successes. I made sleeping on Svart's couch sound like an extended spa-cation, the early practice sessions of me, Svart, and Tomi like a black metal version of Rush, a triumvirate of progressive innovation. I topped it off by pulling out my freshly signed lease.

"I'll be staying awhile. It's a really nice place. It's been great staying with Svart, but I have enough money saved that I can afford to live by myself."

Whether that was actually true remained to be seen, but I knew she'd report back to Juan. Since I wasn't subsidizing puppets and outlandish headwear, I figured I'd be solvent for at least a few months. For the length of the lease. If things got really bad, I could lobby for some parental aid. Guilt my mom, call her and tell her about Mrs. Svart's unconditional support and motivation.

"Svart's mom . . . she's fantastic. Works at the language school. She told me the best year of her life was when she lived abroad. Alone."

"Maybe we can get together? Take something to drink?" she asked.

At first, I thought this was some abstract invite, a suggestion extended for politeness' sake. The kind of thing you ask before leaving. I'm never too sympathetic to the Euro stereotypes of Americans—you know, that we're simultaneously lazy and work-obsessed—though they may be onto something with their claims of our ignorance and self-absorption. On top of that, I would also agree with the common Euro perception that if an American extends an invite, you shouldn't take it seriously.

"Let's have lunch sometime!" doesn't mean tomorrow, the next day, or even the following week. It's just a vague expression of friendliness.

A conditional friendliness: "I'd like to have lunch with you at some indeterminate point in the future, but I'd also like to leave without making you feel that I'm blowing you off."

I'm frequently guilty of this, so when Delphine proposed a drink, I just said, "Sure, sure," and tried to go on my way. I thought the conversation had run its course and I'd emphasized the message I wanted her to take to Juan: David Fosberg is doing fine without you.

I'd forgotten that Belgians, most Europeans really, anyone who is not American, are generally suggesting an actual, and not suppositional, drink when they ask if you want a drink.

She touched my shoulder and added, "Oh, I mean now. See? They're coming."

At that moment, Svart, with Juan in tow, turned the corner by the Vooruit and headed down the street toward us. Svart's swag belly swayed like a pregnant cat's. He seemed to be moving faster than normal. He seemed to be smiling. Juan had on his top hat and his ruffled smock. When he saw Delphine, Juan waved, then pointed at the Indian restaurant—the Shalimar Palace—across the street.

Delphine kind of cooed, like a puffed up pigeon. She waved back, then said, "If you're free now, you can join us. We had plans to meet up once Jurgen finished work."

"Plans?" I wondered what Svart was doing with Juan. And why he was smiling. On top of that, how'd Delphine get away with calling Svart "Jurgen"? Only his mother did that.

I felt defensive: hands off my oaf!

"Yes. I knew he needed another guitarist, so put him in touch with Juan. Juan is liking it here, but he needs to get out. Our place is so small, and he spends all day drawing or making art. It can be claustrophobic. For both of us."

Svart smothered me in a massive bear hug. He lifted me off of the ground and roared in my ear, "Desekration is now complete!"

He set me down, and continued, "This is our second guitarist. I believe you know him. And even better news awaits! I just got off the phone with our new singer. Nordikron, from Astrampsychos, called me at the shop. He heard 'To Winds ov Demise' and wants in. He recognizes its true essence. Ha ha! Come, David. First round is on me! These Indian beers are shit, so weak. We will just have to drink more!"

Nordikron. The name filled my belly with a leaden freeze. A Teutonic Transformer sent from the future to eradicate all life through the force of his inhuman maw. But I didn't want to seem lame. Instead, I gave Svart a high five.

"The first round's already here, man!" I said, and handed him the Jupiler. I wanted him to recognize my true essence. To know conclusively that I'm more fun than Juan and his fusty get ups.

Goat Song Sacrifice

Juan tittered nervously as we slammed the beers. Delphine hadn't trained him in the art of public drinking.

"Sorry, dude," I said, then burped toward his hat. "I only bought these two."

Svart and I tossed our empty beers in a nearby trash can. The plastic bag, too. This was before recycling. Then, we all crossed the street to the Shalimar Palace.

"Glad to see you!" Juan said as we made our way through a choked line of Peugeots.

The awkward coldness I anticipated, Juan regarding me as inferior or undeserving of any degree of cordiality, wasn't there. Instead, he appeared regal. Magnanimous. Above, for example, my juvenile belching. Must be Delphine's influence.

"Yeah. You, too. Belgium, huh?" I gestured around me. At nothing. At everything. The shark gray sky, the quiet hustle of people passing by, the tiny cars, none of them shivering through the force of a booty bass powermix.

"It's not Hialeah, but it'll do."

"I often eat here," Svart interjected. He sprinted ahead of us and opened a dark brown oak door with winding lines carved around each panel. He grabbed a solid metal handle that looked like a bronzed cord of nautical rope and guided us toward a deep booth set in the back corner of the restaurant.

As soon as I sat down, I wondered if I shouldn't have just gone home. Eaten with Svart's mom. And not because of Juan or the prospect of working with Nordikron. I hadn't eaten Indian food in over a year. It reminded me too much of her. Of Natasha. Going to an Indian restaurant, to me, was a couple's activity. A culinary prelude to romance. My meat skewer broiled in her blazing tandoor. The one we always went to was a palace, too. The Punjab Palace.

Juan nudged me with the menu and for once I was thankful he was here. I didn't need to think about Natasha. Regale myself with that crippling lovelorn rhapsody. Again. And if I did, maybe he'd help me out. Give me some advice. He'd always been good at that kind of thing. He'd obviously gotten over his ex-girlfriend. Over Gale. I'd almost forgotten her name.

"So you're staying at Jurgen's, huh? Relying on the largesse of others. It must be instructive. Enlightening, even," he said.

There it was. The little poke acknowledging that he hadn't forgotten. He'd make me pay. Make me apologize. On his schedule, on his terms.

He wasn't going to let me forget it. Well, best to go with it, let bygones be bygones, I thought. Maybe I deserved it?

"Yeah, I'm not fucking him, but he still gives me a place to sleep."

"Not yet anyway," Svart said, and reached over to tweak my nipple.

In a social setting, Svart abandoned the increasingly scolding tone he'd used to talk to me at home. I suppose if you live on someone's couch for long enough, you become like their couch. You become like something they own. Or a pet. Something they can shame when you don't behave accordingly. And praise when you do some trick they taught you.

"But if I buy you some samosas or something, maybe you'll finally start putting out. Ha ha! I'll get some for everyone. Maybe someone'll put out." He leered at Delphine.

"My treat," he added, then waved the waiter over to the table.

The waiter was Indian, around my age. Did he study

Goat Song Sacrifice

Dutch, too? He and Svart gobbled and honked back and forth. The only words I could make out were "samosa," "masala," and "alstublieft," the all-purpose word for "please," "thank you," and about twelve other things. Probably not. This guy's too advanced. Niveau tien at the very least. He came to me and I pointed at a picture of chicken curry.

Bravely, I muttered "kip . . . curry . . . alstublieft."

He smiled and collected our menus. He said something that made Svart and Delphine chuckle, then disappeared behind a cowrie shell curtain leading to the kitchen.

Svart asked Delphine about a few of her friends. How were they doing? Did they ever ask about him? It seemed like he knew a lot about her. After the waiter brought a round of beers for the table, I asked them how they knew each other. I mean, I couldn't really imagine them hanging out.

"What? How do I know Delphine? Ha ha!" He reached across the table, across Juan, and under the table, where he must have pinched her thigh or something because she squirmed involuntarily and her cheeks reddened. Like the ripest lingonberries.

"Everyone knows Delphine!"

She laughed, patted his arm, and gently pushed it away.

"He means I know a lot of people in the music scene. Musicians, writers, label people. I used to promote a lot of shows before I got so involved in my university studies."

"Oh yeah. She used to promote them, all right!" Svart hoisted his Kingfisher, and quickly tipped the bottom toward her.

Juan sat silent, his empty stare framed by the curtains of black hair that hung down from the brim of his top hat. The pink roses in the brim still languished in the throes of decay. He'd tucked a cassette tape into the brim next to them.

He'd changed his costume. I just hadn't noticed at first.

Subtle changes. First, it looked like he'd used a comb, or maybe a pick, to make his hair thick, so that it framed his head like a wide, black penumbra. His hair had been, for lack of a better word, "volumized." He looked like a lustrous brunette in a Vidal Sassoon commercial if, of course, you slapped a mangy top hat on her head.

On top of that, a thick line of mascara framed each eye. Clotted his eyelashes like the feathers of some Exxoned pelican. Maybe that's what he'd been doing for the past month, I thought. Letting Delphine comb his hair and smear his face with makeup. Like she had her own Sisters of Mercy Ken doll.

"No one is bound by what they used to do," he said, and winked at me.

Either that, or he blinked to dislodge an inky eyeliner crumb.

When the food came—bowls of rice, curries, and a small midden of crunchy samosas—Svart turned to business.

"You know Nekrokor too, right?" Svart asked Juan.

Juan suppressed the slightest trace of a grin and slowly blinked.

"Well, I never said I met him."

Who knows what he'd told Svart to edge into the band.

"But I can assure you that I know him," Juan continued. "I know what he's about. What he wants." He picked up a samosa, bit into it, and then put it back on the plate.

"I've studied his music. It would be irresponsible not to."

"That is true." Svart turned serious, leaning forward with both elbows on the table.

"And I think you're right, Jurgen. That's why I wanted to give you this,"

He reached up, fiddled with the brim of his hat, and pulled down the cassette wedged next to the roses.

It wasn't a prop. He'd been working. On something other

than his costume.

"It's a tape. With some ideas. I tried to imagine myself making 'To Winds ov Demise,' Side C. If you extended the last song on the second side, when the last guitar fades into the winter wind, this is how it might sound. Here."

He slid it into Svart's palm. Svart held the tape up to his nose and squinted at it, his nose scrunched up as though he could smell the riffs mustifying into a blackened state of decay. Maybe Juan had seasoned the tape in Delphine's panty drawer?

He'd covered the tape's plastic shell with an elaborate mountainscape rendered with blue ink, Wite-Out, and a silver paint marker.

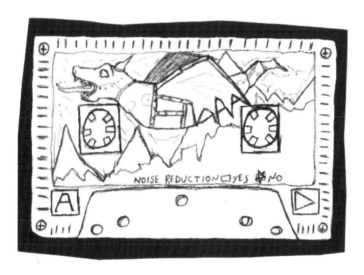

A giant winged something—a bat or a fuzzy snow lizard—hovered over the glaciated peaks.

"It's the . . . what is it called? That dragon?

"The gulden draak?" Delphine suggested. It's a golden dragon on top of one of the towers in the city center.

"That's right. I'm really glad Delphine has a turntable," Juan went on, playing the role of the flattering sophisticate.

"I listen to Desekration all the time. You know, she's at school a lot, so I've got the luxury of time."

"Geen probleem, man. Glad to help."

"And I just want to say that I really appreciate you giving me that record. Anything else you've got, I'd love to listen to it."

He pointed at the samosa plate, where one fried brown triangle remained, "Do you mind?"

"Take it," Svart said. "It's yours."

I sighed loudly, then reached for my beer. Juan remained the same, with or without the makeover.

"Anything less," he said between chews, "shows an unfortunate lack of seriousness."

"Uitstekend, man!" Svart said, then slipped the tape into his pocket.

"I like your initiative. David here, he studies poorly. Music and language. My mom knows his Dutch teacher. She says he is the worst student in the whole class. Can you imagine? The worst. In a class full of future street sweepers and Baltic baby factories. But of course—they have a reason to study. My taxes!"

I just sat there, cradling my half full bottle and picking at the edges of the label.

"Don't worry, though," Svart winked at me and took a swig. "We'll keep you around. For at least a little bit more."

Juan cackled.

"Wait a second. A Dutch class? You live in Miami for twenty years and don't speak Spanish, but you spend a couple of weeks here and sign up for some language immersion program?"

"Yeah, man. I want to stay here. Give it a go. I didn't want to stay there." I told them about the apartment, too. Svart took it well. He just nodded as I talked about it.

When he said, "That's good. Now I've got a place I can bring girls back to," I knew he was cool with it.

After we finished a second round of Kingfishers, the waiter scraped our curried remains into a few to-go containers. Svart and Delphine divided the bill, then we left.

At the top of the hill, Svart and I split off. Delphine and Juan headed toward the city center. Apparently, she lived in some old apartment out by a castle called Gravensteen on the other side of town.

Before we left, Juan said, "Here. I probably owe you."

He shook his leftovers, a few naan shards and a lump or two of curry sauce, like an oversized Styrofoam rattle.

"Consider it a housewarming gift."

"Carry mine, too," Svart said. He rested his on top, leaving me to balance a stack of squeaky containers set to unlatch at the slightest jostle and catapult passersby with a hail of rice flecks.

"You still my bitch. Until you move out, you got to work for your meal."

8.
Summer Dying Fast

"Dude, why didn't you tell me about Juan?" I asked Svart as we headed back to his house. I wasn't sure I was ready to put up with the guy again. I'd enjoyed my time off.

"Well, now you know," he said. "Now he's in. Nordikron, too."

"Yeah, right. Him too. I thought that guy was in, you know, Astrampsychos."

"I thought so as well. I didn't get to talk to him for too long. It sounded like he'd called from a payphone. In a supermarket or something. The connection was very bad. He said he's done with that. He's done with Astrampsychos and he heard we needed a singer. That's all I needed. I offered him the spot. I'm not going to turn down the best voice of our time."

The overcast afternoon had faded into a fog-gray evening. We passed the goth pub. De Verloren Hemel. The one with the pierced barmaid. Then, we crossed the Leie River—a body of water only slightly wider than a canal—and walked down the Coupure Links along a brick bike path flanked on each side by tall trees. The dense leaves cloaked us. It felt like we'd disappeared into the forest. Overhead, finches fluttered deeper into the branches as we walked by. They sensed the squeak of my stack of Styrofoam leftovers as some predatory wail.

"How'd he know that?" I asked.

"Like I told you, man. He must have heard 'To Winds.' There's no other way. He heard it and recognized its supremacy."

"Yeah ..." I had a hard time believing this, but I didn't have a better explanation.

"Here. Let me show you something."

Svart stepped off the bike path and into the grass. A bicyclist streamed past, the bike's pedal-powered headlight strobing into the night. Svart put his hand on my shoulder and guided me around the trunk of one of the trees.

"You recognize this tree?" he asked.

Before I could answer, he went on.

"It's on the cover of 'To Winds.'"

I looked up into a thick cloud of leaves. A few agitated birds squawked down in disapproval. I couldn't believe him. This couldn't be the same icy tree skeleton, the spiked labyrinth of frozen branches, splayed across its cover.

"And this ..."

He stuck his fingers in a grooved gash in the bark.

"Look at it," he said. He traced the contours of a pentagram he'd carved, he told me, "for future historians."

He'd carved it into the tree trunk the day he'd picked up

the first batch of pressed copies of "To Winds." I touched it too, the dried sap as smooth as blown glass.

"I knew I'd made something for the ages," he said. "Something that will be around even longer than this tree."

In my last few days of couch surfing, I resolved to be a team player. To do what Svart wanted me to do. I restrung my guitar and used my keyboard to tune it properly. I would no longer follow the well-trod path of downtuned distortion. Quit fucking around, David, I thought as I turned the pegs, strummed a string, then matched the sound against the most basic guitar tone on the synthesizer. Just play it right. Move into the apartment. Don't blow it. I was still a bit shocked that Juan was, once again, my bandmate. Though it hadn't really registered at the time, I couldn't stop dwelling on Svart's offhand joke about kicking me out. He hadn't said anything like that to Juan, even though he was barely distinguishable from the Verloren Hemel regulars Svart heckled every time we went in there. It pissed me off so much I didn't just de-downtune my guitar. I uptuned it. Twisted the pegs a bit too tight. Added a half step to a half step. A full step. I wanted it to make the shrillest banshee shriek imaginable. A rusty chainsaw's limb-rending whine. I wanted it to sound like Nordikron's voice.

If Svart weren't so dumb, I'd say he did it on purpose. That he put Juan in the band just to piss me off. Incite me to perform. Show me I'm disposable. And give him one additional connection, imagined or not, to Despondent Abyss. To Nekrokor.

After I finished, the guitar felt taut, tight. Like each string would snap, scorpion-strike my eye, if I dared touch it. When Svart came home later that afternoon, I greeted him with a wailing flagellation of the lead in "Winterminion Ensorcels." We still didn't have any other songs. He put down his bag, and nodded his head.

"Good, I see you've been studying," he finally said. "Your guitar. Working on its accent."

The morning of the move, I woke up to rain so hard I could hear each drop hitting the roof two floors above me. By the time I'd had some coffee and a piece of toast with jam, the rain hadn't eased up. In addition to a collared shirt, I thought, I should probably invest in a rain jacket. Or a waterproof parka if I really wanted to plan ahead.

Svart's door was still closed. He'd gone out with Juan and Tomi the night before. I wasn't bummed about it. He'd left a note for me. I'd been out buying practical things, household essentials—a bath towel, a couple washcloths, a set of bedsheets. I even sprung for a coffee maker. Home is where the hearth is. The gallons of free coffee I'd swilled as a Booksalot peon had turned me into a junkie. If I didn't have any within an hour or so of waking up, a massive anaconda of a headache steadily constricted my skull until I secured the antidote. The poison.

I rooted under the sink and pulled out a sleeve of white garbage bags. I bagged the guitar, the keyboard, stuffed my backpack with the towels and sheets along with things like hand lotion and toothpaste, and slipped it on. Then, I pulled a garbage bag over my head and around the swollen hump of my backpack. I ripped a hole for my face. The bag's creased corner tented over my forehead.

I checked my pocket for the apartment key, then went outside. It rained harder as I stepped out onto the street, like I'd punctured the clouds with my head. Rain streamed down the peak of my plastic cowl, over the crest of my backpack, and pooled in my shoes.

Head down, I hustled across the street and over to the Coupure Links, the bike path that ran by Svart's place. I thought I'd be drier once I made it under the trees, but even there, the rain drove down hard on my Glad Bag poncho. I scampered down the bike path, trying to cover the distance as fast as possible, then stopped when I got to Svart's carved tree. Of course it wasn't dry under the trees. The leaves were gone. A soggy clump of mulch, a wet hill of brown leaves, cir-cled the tree trunk. It wasn't high enough to cover Svart's en-graving, his monument to the forthcoming dark age, but it was nearly as high as my knee. There hadn't been any leaves on the ground before. Not even the night before when I came back from shopping. The same fate had befallen every tree. Not just the one Svart had marked. It hadn't suddenly keeled over from the force of his maleficent glyph. They'd all died. Shed their leaves. Overnight. So this, I thought, is why they called it "fall." I mean, they weren't really dead. You know that. Trees lose their leaves, then grow them again. No big deal. But I'd never seen it happen. I didn't think they'd fall so quickly. So soon. All at once. And me, wearing only a garbage bag. Single ply.

No birds huddled for warmth in the sharp spiral of deleafed branches. They'd been dispersed, frozen, or other-wise wiped out by the winds of demise. Suddenly Svart's nonsensical title made sense. The cover picture, too. The forks and spiny brachiations of the branches were more like the bone lattice of bat wings, the skeletal wings of a skeleton-ized brood, than anything green and living.

It's not quite true that there weren't any birds. One bird, its feathers puffed around it into a gray orb, perched, unmov-ing. I didn't notice it at first. I mistook it for some knobbed canker, the elbow of a disjointed branch.

It peeped once, then shuddered, shaking off a hazy cloud of mist.

I pulled my hood low over my nose and continued walking. I had to stop every ten steps or so to readjust my grip on the keyboard, then the guitar, then the keyboard again, wet plastic slipping over wet plastic. I limped across the bridge, past De Verloren Hemel, up the hill, past the Record Huis, and down to Rooseveltlaan, the keyboard teetering on one thigh, the guitar slowly pulling my arm from its socket, the straps of my overstuffed backpack gripping my neck in a sustained Vulcan pinch.

If you saw me, stumbling through the rain, you'd think I was the hunchbacked devotee of some spiritualist sect. Golden Dawn or some splinter group. A pilgrim in white robes. Through the gray porridge of a crappy Belgian morning, my instruments and I may have been mistaken for three pilgrims. A trio bundled together with red drawstrings for some penitential circuit of the city.

When I got to the apartment, I closed the door and locked it. I stripped off the plastic bag, my shoes, and the rest of my clothes. Alone at last, I fished the hand lotion out of my backpack.

9.
Housewarmings

I got the first one a few days after I moved in. A housewarming gift. From Nekrokor. Sent with love.

A row of steel mailboxes lined the building's lobby. In Belgium, they deliver the mail in the morning. I was on my way to Dutch class. Showered and freshly scrubbed so I'd smell good for the Azerbabe. Don't want her to get morning sickness, hurl on my workbook. I saw the mailman stick an envelope into the mailbox marked with my apartment number. My mailbox. I hadn't checked it until then.

Who would write me? As far as I knew, no one had the address. Just Svart and his mom.

The mailman locked the box. He gave me a nod and an "Alstublieft!" before he moved down the row. This "alstublieft" conveyed, I think, his assurance that my mail would remain secure until I sprung it out of the box.

I rifled through my front pocket for my keys, popped open the mailbox, and pulled out a single postcard. Under the dim track lighting in the lobby, I couldn't make out much more than a dark color block. I bid the mailman a muffled but competent "Goeiedag," then stepped out into another dismal morning on the Rooseveltlaan. The sky hovered overhead, as gray and massive as the vast belly of some gargantuan brachiosaurus.

Need to buy a jacket, I thought, as I did each time I stepped outside. I glanced at the postcard. Even under the morning light, I had a hard time seeing much more than a flat field of black. Maybe I need to buy glasses too, I wondered, squinting as I made out two purple columns near the center of the postcard. A light mist settled on the card's glossy surface.

I flipped it over and read a short message:

Thinking of you.
—N.

A hyphen and an initial. N. Nekrokor, of course. Thinking of you. That's all he wrote. In neat block letters. I mean, I guess there was a bit more than that. In the upper left corner, it gave the name of the painting, "Black on Maroon," and the artist. Mark Rothko. It listed the location, too. The Tate in London. The stamp confirmed it. A mosaic face of Jesus. He'd stuck it on upside down. I read the postmark. He'd sent it a few days before. Shelled out thirty-nine pence to send me a black rectangle.

From what I knew of Nekrokor, cultural refinement wasn't exactly his thing. Maybe he'd been scouting out covers for another Astrampsychos album? *Live in Brno II: Crucifixion Boogaloo*. The lines in the painting looked like a Roman numeral two. Or windows. If you were trapped in a tower, some medieval colossus designed to stave off an invasion of crusading Frisians, this might be what you'd see. Twin slivers just the right size for aiming a notched arrow, but too narrow to let one in. Twin windows looking out on a blooddawn the color of a shriveled eggplant. Through cataracts.

Cataract blooddawn. A good song title. Have to run it by Svart, I thought.

Svart—that's who probably gave him my address. Maybe while making arrangements to bring the new singer to town.

And what he wrote—thinking of you?

Thinking I needed to get to work, probably. Thinking he wanted to jab me with that knife of his. Two gashes in me, bleeding purple, just like the Rothko. The more I thought about it, the more it seemed like exactly the kind of thing Nekrokor would send to me. Like that letter he'd sent me in Miami. The envelope filled with toxic slime. Threatening, yes, but ultimately nothing to worry about. At least the guy was making an effort to communicate.

The next one came in a padded envelope. A few days later. He'd sent it from Brussels. It had a stamp of a bird with its head turned, an eye facing out. A less frozen version of the one roosting in Svart's tree monument. Right side up, too. No cryptophilatelic messaging that I could discern.

I gently squeezed the envelope. My fingers probed the contours of something small and solid inside, maybe some kind of souvenir, a Rothko magnet or—since he sent it from Brussels—a little Manneken Pis or something, a mischievous cherub to piss on my head. I squeezed a bit harder. It felt rounded, like the hood of a tiny toy Porsche, and pliable, something made of plastic or rubber. I snorted. A souvenir? This is Nekrokor we're talking about. More like a beheaded Manneken Pis. Or a single-serv packet of poisonous jelly. A do-it-yourself suicide kit. I squeezed again. I didn't want any unpleasant surprises.

Something gave way, just a little, beneath my fingers. A tiny crunch. I peeled open the envelope and peeked inside. No letter. No postcard. No obvious biohazards, either.

Goat Song Sacrifice

I reached in and pulled out something jumbled and spiky. Something brown and clumpy. Like a handful of mashed raisins. A couple of toothpicks, too. The raisins skewered to the toothpicks. A high fiber fruit kabob. I shook the envelope to dislodge anything else in there. A lone bit of string, a paintbrush bristle or a stray hair, fell into my palm.

An antenna.

I pinched one of the toothpicks between my fingers and raised it up. I hoisted the whole mass. An opaque glob of superglue as hard and pitted as calcified snot held the whole thing together. It joined the toothpicks in a cross.

And the brown glob? He hadn't sent me raisins. Just the raisin-brown body of a dead cockroach. I wondered where he'd found it. I didn't think they lived in Europe. Too nice. Too temperate. They preferred, I knew from personal experience, to swarm in droves around the crumbs and Lucky Charms bits strewn in Miami cupboards. It was an exotic. Invasive. Like me.

He'd impaled the roach on one of the toothpicks. The point poked through the head and came out of the abdomen. Its bent legs folded neatly, nearly overlapping, like a six-armed Dracula in coffined repose.

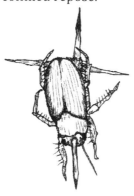

He'd crucified it. Upside down. Its lone antenna hung limply.

The mailman gave me a weird look as I stepped outside. No "Alstublieft" today. He'd been watching me. I'm officially the guy who gets dead bug care packages.

I examined this latest "gift" from Nekrokor. I held it in the air as I walked down the Rooseveltlaan. The Belgian grandmas, normally so circumspect and adept at ignoring the existence of everyone but their little dogs, peered openly at me and the thing in my hands.

There goes the neighborhood.

He'd impaled it on a purple toothpick. He'd somehow stained the head of the toothpick cross the same color as the windows or whatever on the Rothko postcard. Maroon.

He hadn't stained it, I realized. I had. With my blood. I'd seen that toothpick before. In Trondheim. When I first met Nekrokor. I'd put it in my mouth. Used it to jab a cheese cube. Used it to jab my palm, too. And then smear a beer coaster with my blood. He'd taken the coaster, then stuck it in a pocket of his zipper-spangled leather jacket. He'd said, "Don't break the oath," then headed off to bone some girl. And here it was again. Another reminder. A second reminder.

I should probably get in touch with this guy, I thought. He knows where I am. A cold breeze rattled the roach carcass like a tiny maraca. One of the legs snapped off and spun down to the sidewalk. The further dismemberment of the already defiled bug. It had lost two appendages since I'd opened the envelope. The poor dead bug. It wasn't safe.

I wasn't safe either. Brussels lay a short train ride away. And the street swarmed with eyes. Not just Belgian grandmas and their dogs. I started to feel paranoid. Was I the roach? Had I somehow, in the nekroconvoluted logic of Nekrokor's mind, broken the oath? Across the street, a thicket of leafless branches shook in the wind. He could be there, I thought. Crouched and poised to strike at any moment. Above me, the curtains rustled in an apartment window. He could be there, too. Ready to push open the window and drop down on my back. Rambo blade first.

I tucked the bug back in the envelope. He knows where I am, I thought and hurried to class.

I tried not to think about it. I went to class. Came home. Went on long walks. I talked myself out of my paranoia. No one leaped out of the thicket at me, or assailed me in the street.

It's true, I reasoned, that Nekrokor could be in Brussels. But he'd just been in London. And Norway before that. This guy, in his Eurowanderings, could have been anywhere. For all I knew, he could have been in Miami, fêting Natasha at a Pollo Tropical.

He could have been anywhere, but I had no reason to fear that he could be in Gent. My neighborhood. Haunting the Rooseveltplein. I believed that more with each passing day. And even if he were, I had no reason to think he wished me ill. Among black metal crazies, a gift of impaled vermin could mean any number of things. It could be a show of support. A commentary on European immigration policies. A coded message revealing the sales figures of the latest Astrampsychos release.

Six legs plus one antenna equals seven copies sold.

I filled my refrigerator with Belgian beers and, sometimes, food. In the evenings, I drank in Svartless silence. I sat in the part of my one room apartment most like a living room. A black and red rag rug marked off a tiny chill zone between the bed and the radiator grille. It's where I kept my guitar and keyboard. The rug reminded me of one we had in our den when I was a kid, but I hadn't seen any like it since Ronald Reagan took office. A real chair wouldn't fit on it, but there was some kind of Eurorecliner, part bean bag, part orthopedic wedge pillow, with room to spare for a side table just wide enough for a few Jupiler cans. The pillowchair was covered in dark brown velvet. It had a crescent shape, so you could rock back and forth while swigging beers. It looked like a soft sculpture of a rotting banana. I'm sure you could find a similar model marketed somewhere as a marital aid.

A few beers in, I figured I should probably eat something.

One tomato, simultaneously rotten and frozen, sat in the butter tray. A hunk of petrified cheese. Several Jupiler blikjes flanked a foam takeout box. I pulled it out and popped the lid. Chicken curry with fossilized naan fragments. Juan's leftovers. I took a bite, savoring a chicken chunk marinated in a musty carbonated fizz. Carbonated. Carbonized. Like Han Solo. Preserved forever. Just need a little heat to bring it back through a kind of pasteurization. I shrugged and switched on the oven.

I scooped the curry into a metal pan and stuck it in the oven. I pulled open the patio door and stepped outside while I waited. It started to rain. Across the courtyard, an old lady came out onto her terrace. She pulled a bunch of beige bras and towels off a drying rack, then retreated inside. It rained some more.

I went back in, spooned the curry into a bowl, then took it over to the pillowchair. I balanced the bowl in my lap. The curve of the bowl grazed the curve of my belly. The curve of my belly, I noticed, exhaling and pushing it out to its max, had reached a greater max, a broader circumference. Too many beers. Too many friets. And the shitty weather's not helping matters, I thought. No sunny strolls among prehistoric banyans, humid evenings to heat the blood. No dip into the pisswarm ocean on a day off from work. True, I missed my annual bout of testicular heat rash, but, sitting alone, the heavy gloom outside, the rain pelting the building, it seemed a heavy price to pay. And the ocean, so far away. An hour by train. It felt so far even though if I went outside and tasted the raindrops, I could still detect the faintest tang of salt.

"More salt," I mumbled, walked over to the kitchen, and showered my putrescent leftovers. Anything to mask the fizzy taste. Like pop rocks. Chicken-flavored pop rocks. I continued munching. Chicken curry. It made me think of Natasha. I know. I know. I needed to get over her. Believe me, I tried. The Azerbabe, getting more pregnant by the day, was off limits, but I had my eye on a Romanian girl who always hung around after class smoking cigarettes. She had hairy arms, though, and a goblin shark smile. I'd seen a few rocker chicks in the city, too. Baby steps. It's just that chicken curry reminded me of the final days of my relationship with Natasha. The end of her reign.

It reminded me of the Punjab Palace, one of our Friday night mainstays. I'd pick her up from her parents' house, take her there for samosas and curry, and try to lay the groundwork for getting up her batik print skirt before her 1 AM curfew. Life was simple then. My goals clear and direct.

It shared the strip mall with a fairly typical assortment of Miami businesses: an autoparts chain, an exotic reptile store called We've Got Herps, and, right next door, a head shop/adult movie combo called Swampy Style that billed itself as "The Place for Your Tobacco and Independent Video Needs." If you didn't catch the euphemisms, their sign cleared it all up: a cartoonish alligator with bloodshot eyes and a fat joint dangling from its mouth grappled the scaly flanks of another alligator with flowing blond ringlets. Swampy Style. Get it?

Inside the Punjab Palace, you couldn't tell that you were

just a few inches, a few sheets of particle board, away from endless rows of videos depicting every sexual permutation imaginable, buy three get one free. How do I know this? After the breakup, let's just say I drove to the Punjab Palace for the lunch buffet, thought better of it, and before you knew it, found myself conducting an independent examination of Swampy Style's inventory.

It's a wonder I ever bothered to take her anywhere else. Tapestries made from the same material as Natasha's skirts—mustard yellow, terra cotta, and spangled with tiny round mirrors and metal beads—displayed an entire range of Hindu divinities, many engaged in the same kind of antics as the alligators next door. Elephant men and three-headed gods, each one cupped his consort's basketball breasts and gave her the old swampy style, standing up, while she grasped an ankle and hoisted a leg over her head.

When you've paid, stand out in the parking lot with a blunted gator in flagrante delicto above you and you ask, "So, now what should we do?" you get ideas. And so does your wispy girlfriend, even though she once wanted to see if Swampy Style carried the latest Almodóvar film.

The last time I ate at the Punjab Palace, I went with some blonde I met at the Booksalot help desk. I picked up her phone number after I guided her to book twelve of some romance series. *The Baby-Sitters Club*, repackaged for postpubescents. I had to, I felt, because I could. It was so easy.

After we ate, the girl suggested we go back to my place. I agreed. I rolled past the front of my apartment building, angling for an empty parking spot down the street. Natasha sat on the front steps. Her eyes followed the car. Should have tinted the windows, I thought.

I palmed the girl's head and thrust it toward my lap. If this chick moved fast enough, I figured, Natasha might not see her golden hair—practically fluorescent under the street-light glare.

"What are you doing?" she squealed, then ducked under and away from my hand with a fluid shrug. "I had a nice time, but I don't really know you yet," she said, then flicked her hair over her shoulder.

"Oh. I. I wasn't . . ." I laughed nervously. She'd interpreted the crotchward movement of her face as my attempt at fore-play. My timing disappointed her more than the action itself.

"You know, I'd really like you to take me home now," she said. She leaned as far away from me as possible. She rested her head against the passenger side window.

Natasha stood on the sidewalk, staring into the car as I drove past. She could probably read the clock in the car.

"Yeah, that's what we're doing," I muttered.

I sped to the corner and turned off my street. I dropped the blonde off and drove back home. This took about half an hour. No goodnight kiss.

When I came back, Natasha still sat on the front stairs. Waiting. She'd seen the girl. And that's how it ended. I mean, I'll spare you the tears, the part where she socked me in the nose, the part where she ran wildly down the street scream-ing and crying, even though those are the moments I brooded over, munching my curry, until I finished eating and went to sleep.

I was so stupid.

Midway through the night, I woke up sweating, the sheets as damp as the moist toilettes I'd used before bed to wipe the curry sauce from my fingers. The sudden dilation of my sphincter roused me awake. I sniffed, then grimaced. An allu-vial fart miasma hovered over the futon. My ass spasmed again, unloosing a single drop of slurry from its floodgates.

The curry.

Just the thought of its crusted edges, the tepid chicken chunks in the middle, and a single squirt of acrid saliva spritzed across my tongue.

The kind you get before you barf.

I leaped off the sheets and planted myself, face first, by the toilet. I tentatively dipped my nose past the rim of the toilet and waited, like a fisherman. Don't they chum the water first, to entice the fish? I imagined the sound of fish bits splattering on water. I pulled my face out of the toilet and rested on the cool tiles.

I caught a glimpse of a dirty napkin in the wastebasket and hunched back over the toilet. Shalimar Palace, I curse your name.

It was not a restful night.

10.
Het Ziekenhuis

I eased in and out of full-scale delirium for almost a week. I still made it to class, paying diligent attention to the new chapter, Les Zes: Het Ziekenhuis, but hadn't managed to eat any actual food. Svart called one day to tell me the new singer would be in town that weekend. I told him I'd be ready to meet the guy.

At school, I asked my teacher for help, advice, maybe even sympathy. When I told her about the curry, all she could do was laugh.

"Americans," she muttered. "So, food doesn't rot in America or something?"

The other students nodded knowingly on one of our breaks. Old chicken, I learned, was never safe. I should have realized that my waist-high refrigerator didn't cool as well as a full-size one. Plus, hardly anyone ate chicken. Everyone, from Belgians to Spaniards to transient Uzbekies, knew it was a "dirty food."

Three days later, and I still couldn't manage solid food. A single bite of anything produced simultaneous oral and anal detonations minutes after I swallowed. My teacher, still marveling at the stupidity of a nation of self-poisoners, pointed me to the Glucozade machine down the hall. Watery and with a barely discernible flavor, like a half-Gatorade, half-water mix for the price of two Gatorades, the Glucozade sustained me through my classes.

At night, the fever and chills returned. I spent hours on the toilet, imagining the tiles to be a chessboard that a lone knight leapfrogged as my anus disgorged a gelatinous Glucozadal mass. Sometimes, in mid shit, I'd kneel on the floor, my bare ass in the air, and bellow my wretched vomit cry directly onto a slippery discharge of rectal slime. Then, spittle on my face, I'd flop on the bed, running through vocabulary lists in my mind, typing the letters against my chest—ziekenhuis, ziekenwagen, ziekelijk.

I needed these words. Sickhouse. Sickwagon. Sicklike. I'd imagine dialogues from the chapter, but make them fit my situation:

"Waar ligt het ziekenhuis? Ik heb _____. Wilt u mij helpen?" The book had a bunch of words to fill in—things like "hoofdpijn" and "een gebroken arm"—but no ready-made phrase for my pathetic state. The best thing I could think of was "een groot diarree"—"a big diarrhea."

I'd picture helpful Belgian matrons tucking me into their wire grocery carts and wheeling me to the ziekenhuis if I could have summoned the strength to leave the apartment and seek their aid. They knew where it was—it had to be just around the corner or something. I sensed I was within a five-minute carting of advanced medical care. I'd seen the hospital bus as I hauled myself to and from class. It was clearly marked—Z18: Ziekenhuis. I tried to spur my legs into action, tried to get up and out of my apartment, until I fell asleep, fell into the grip of another salmonella vision.

Asleep in another room.

Goat Song Sacrifice

Another time.

No, not asleep, but tossing through a sweaty 3 AM fever. Like this one. A stomach flu. But not from chicken curry. Spaghetti. When I was a kid. My stomach gurgled and I ran to the bathroom from the den. I pushed back my wooden TV tray and left just as Hannibal and Murdock successfully drugged Mr. T as part of some masterful plan. I ran to the bathroom, but I didn't make it. A spicy ragout of chewed meatballs and, well, Ragú exploded out of my mouth and across the doorway instead. And then I got really sick. Delusional sick. Feverish and tucked in with a Pepto Bismol nightcap, I stared at the lines separating the gray plane of the roof from the gray plane of the wall, the shifting lines, the shifting planes. Nausea spread through my body and into my mind.

Dad really should have fried those meatballs a bit longer.

Like now, my curry. We are doomed to repeat the sins of the father.

The walls tilted and the tiled floor, a monochrome chessboard as gray as everything else, climbed up the wall. Lying on my back, the ceiling, the floor, the walls, emanated from the single corner I stared into. Somehow the window stayed even, the sill stubbornly parallel to the flat ground I knew had to exist outside. Maybe its connection to the outside freed it from the sickening geometry of the room? I wanted to throw up again, but I knew I'd never make it.

I'd roll down the floor, down the hall, like a big undercooked meatball, and miss the bathroom entirely.

Instead, I stared out the window, its non-kaleidoscoping shape floodlit by my neighbor's security lights, installed as a direct response to the DEA's recent community information campaign. As everyone knew, drug gangs and crazed Santeros roamed the dense mile of mangrove swamp that separated our development from Biscayne Bay.

I reasoned that if I stared long enough, the window would transmit its correct proportions through the light beams. The other half of my fevered young mind replayed the opening measures of C.P.E. Bach's "Solfeggietto," in an endless loop:

Right middle, left pinky, left middle, left thumb, right thumb, right pinky, right ring, right middle, right index . . .

My fingers marked out the opening notes against my *Empire Strikes Back* comforter.

I guess I thought the proportions of the notes would somehow offset the room's chaos. I used to play that song over and over again, as fast as possible. I still do. When I'm sick, tired, or hungover, the song streams through my mind. I drummed the notes, fixated on the one stable point in a shifting room gone askew.

And then it appeared. Backlit by the blazing security beacon, a creature glared at me from the windowsill. It had no eyes, but I knew it stared at my hands. My parents did that when they wanted me to stop playing. They called it a "nervous habit."

The creature, a birdlike shadow with a body like a black felt barrel, appeared unperturbed by the room's jarring asymmetry. Its crooked carrot beak chattered like a pelican's.

And this is the ridiculous part, the reason I keep this memory to myself, but return to it every time I feel sick and dizzy, drag it out like some old tear stained love letter from

Goat Song Sacrifice

Natasha: it was Gonzo, you know, the Muppet.

It was Gonzo if Jim Henson had made him entirely from bristly black pipe cleaners and left off the googly eyes.

Sheer terror for a little kid.

I stopped my piano-less playing. Its voice, flat and high-pitched, told me I would run out of notes in my lifetime. Everyone would. That would stop the playing.

The eyeless beaked shadow clattered, "There will be no more new songs to play. The combinations are limited."

That night in Gent, I knew I was alone. The perennial autumn rain pattered the windowsill. Too cold for Muppets. And I knew it was right. We were near the end. There will be no more new songs to play. Total death reigns eternally.

At some point in the night, I put on every single piece of clothing I owned. My jacket, five shirts, even some socks for my hands. I shivered wildly. I shook like Nekrokor's dead roach probably did when he stabbed it. As the night slogged on, my fevered brain moved past childhood memories, past "Solfeggietto," and into an ongoing telephone game of recycled riffs that moved in a continuous spiral from Sabbath to Carcass, Metallica to Megadeth, Iron Maiden to Iron Maiden, and back to Sabbath again.

This is how they will find me, I thought, imagining that any sound coming through the window had to be the bus to the hospital. This is how they'll find me, load me up, and drop me in the earth.

What's the word for cemetery? I wondered, as I drifted through my fever catacomb, another good song title.

11.
Metametal:
The Nekronomikon Eucharist

Once a year the white robes go on a quest
In search of a virgin, a child of innocence
Born of Apollon divine is the heritage
Chosen by foe to accomplish a holy task
—Candlemass, "Bearer of Pain"

I am one of many. Legion. We are legion. Nameless. Faceless. We share a single robe. Its many cowls rise like the snowy peaks of some forgotten mountain range. No seams separate my robe from that of my companions before me, to my left, to my right, or behind. We've been sewn together. We move together, interlocked. Pilgrims in procession. We have always been one.

We are male and female. Human and animal. All of us bewitched. The waist-high, peaked hood ahead and to my right seems to have two fabric triangles sewn to the side to fit the ears of a wolf or a sheep. Perhaps they cover horns? To my side, a series of hoods, a bit too elongated for the head of any mammal, flails like the tentacles of an agitated hydra.

Goat Song Sacrifice

Our voices shake the ground with the combined force of operatic baritones, pubescent sopranos, even growls and tusky chattering. We sing the same song. The song of our quest. This strange tune possesses our minds.

Its words are found in one sacred book. The Nekronomikon. A vast repository of life. Of total death. Our robes are its pages. We come from, we circle back toward, a city I barely remember, though we are close enough, now, to make out that city's central tower in the distance. We come from a city I barely remember, and the further we travel, our forgetfulness grows into pain.

It pains us to forget that city. We remember it in random flashes that we sing to the others to ease their pain, to lighten their burden of woe. We sing of a tower overlooking the market square. We sing of a chamber at the top of the tower. Someone sings the song of a hag driven mad by the woeful songs of the townspeople, the laments of their livestock. And we remember: yes, she healed their wounds.

She healed our wounds.

Madness heals all wounds and we descend on that city. We've reached it at last. We're returning once again. We have never left it, in truth. Our omnibody stretches across the road, its hem snagged here and there on brush, on tufts of wiregrass. We cross the gentle arc of a stone bridge leading to the market square. Leading to the tower, the chamber, where she waits.

Our combined mass is wider than the bridge. In our eagerness to get to the tower, some of us swim across the canal spanned by the bridge, our robes billowing in the water like the pseudopods of some colossal amoeba, its body as white and creamy as the nape of the maiden's neck when we saw her last, as white and creamy as the cataracts of the crone she had replaced.

As the last ones emerge from the canal, the daggled fringes of their robes brushing the flagstones with muddy streaks, the first of our multitude reach the tower, thinking only of its lone occupant. We think of her as she thinks of us.

We never escape her thoughts.

Together, we gather like some inverse shadow at the tower's base. One of us produces a key, clasps it in a hand, a claw, a talon, and unlocks the door. We enter, nearly all of us, except for a group gathered around a child, the new priestess. We go into the darkness; no, we leave the light.

We flow, together, a stream of bleached blood, upward through the darkness, the twining stair shaft, a spiral artery. Within, the darkness embraces, accentuates, the shuffling of feet, the slap of flippers, the labored breaths of those nearest the chamber door at the top of the tower. A thick slab of birch, battered and worn a bluish gray; the door has no handle, no lock, only what looks like a circular peephole bored through its exact center.

No one expects to see her eye peer through. Our priestess is far beyond that. Instead, a single feather secreted away in some hidden pocket emerges. Secreted away in my pocket. I found the feather at the base of the tower, saw it flutter out of the sky as a pair of vultures circled the chamber. There are always vultures when we open the tower. They have their uses; they know when they are needed.

I hold it by its blue-black vane and jab the quill into the eyehole. The tip punctures something—some filmy membrane resists before it gives way. Then, the opening clenches the shaft, like some voracious mouth, some obscene osculum, and pulls it in, inch by inch, with the sloppy suction of a thorough and full-throated fellating, until the mouth's quivering edges begin to root at my featherless fingertips.

I drop my hand. The door creaks open. An awful stench—

an unholy fart, a bestial queef—hangs like fog. The grimed air begrimes our white robes gray. Despite the smell, we inch in, collectively, through the doorway. She waits, hunched, in the center of the room. Marked by her burden, she suffers for our pain. Last year, she could have been the twin of our child priestess below. Now, wrinkled and tottering, she is older than the oldest among us. Splotches of dried blood cake her desiccated skin. She murmurs words we cannot hear. We embrace her, swallow her in our robes, and lead her to her reward.

An open book rests on a lectern against the far wall. Some kind of writing, the letters raised like a winding line of scabs, crusts across the left hand page. The script scrolls like a schoolgirl's, but the message comes from each of us: "This is my body," written once and centered at the top, like the title of an assigned composition.

We produce a knife from somewhere in our robed horde. It passes from hand to hand or paw to hand to beak to talon, which is to say that all of us touch the handle. The blade slices the page where she wrote her message, our commandment, the law.

The page passes, torn bit by bit, as we hand it down the staircase where the new priestess waits. She will not read the message. It will be gone before it reaches her. Through our pain, she will produce it anew.

I grab the page, pinch a piece, and flatten it in my palm—the letter "i," the dot a globby heart. I place the scrap on my tongue and swallow.

Part Four

O, it grieves my soul that I must draw this metal from my side. . .
—Shakespeare, *King John* (5.2.15-16)

Prisoners of our bodies . . . we aspire to the light.
—Samael, "After the Sepulture"

12.
Singer Phenomenon

Morning stretched its fingers through my wine dark drapes. Sweat boiled down my armpits, steamed my balls like stir fry vegetables. A pounding rattled the windows.

Was it the Z18, the hospital express, come to take me to heaven?

I touched my forehead, greased with sweat and hot as the ass of a Chernobyl whore. Was it my head, that pounding? I heard it again.

Domm domm domm

I heard it, didn't feel it. The noise came from outside this body cocooned in clothes, swaddled for the tomb. The pounding, like muffled words, "Pound . . . pound" and "domm . . . domm," came from the door. Stretching out of bed, I moved hesitantly toward the sound. I still couldn't believe that the sound was something I could move toward, and not a continual pounding generated by the salmonella within. Somehow, I'd survived the night.

I'd been healed. I touched my head, my stomach, my

heart, mystified by my sudden painlessness. I pried myself out of the layers of shirts I'd piled on myself in the night, then opened the door to find Svart, cursing, his fist back for another round of pounding.

"Godverdomme! What you doing in there, man? Verdomme."

He charged in, followed by Juan, who added, "We've been standing out here forever." Well, really, he said, "We've been standing out here forev-ugh," before he clenched his sleeve to his face and strode through the apartment to open the patio door.

Svart grabbed my shoulders and grimaced, a vertical line stretching from his nose to his hairline.

"Verdomme ... you look awful. And all these clothes." He kicked the trail of fabric stretching from the door to the bed. Then he sniffed, his nostrils flared as wide as the openings of some Neolithic cave.

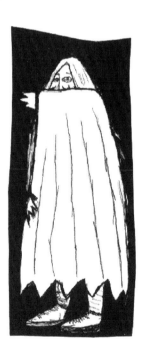

"It smells like shit in here. Godverdomme. You really falling apart, man."

"It's so hot," I muttered, and dropped another shirt on the floor.

A third guy was with them. He had on a cape for, like, Halloween. It could have been from a Batman costume. It was some kind of polyester or vinyl composite, as shiny as a new shower curtain. Its scalloped hem barely reached his waist.

This guy stood directly in front of me holding his cape so it covered half his face. Short and wiry, he barely reached my shoulder even though he had on a pair of thick-soled black boots, their round caps lined with scuffs. He barely reached my shoulder even though, not quite believing I'd been healed, I still walked hunched over, hand on my stomach, as I had for the last week.

He slowly lowered his cape and held his hands at his sides. The dude was old. Way older than the rest of us. He had a pinched face and a sharp beak of a nose. Thick lines—you couldn't call them smile lines, they were more like scowl lines—creased down past the corners of his thin, ash colored lips. They framed his nose and mouth with the dual scythe crescents of some indiscernible band logo, Abruptum or Enthroned. His hair, blond and frizzy, had never recovered from a near fatal nekroperm administered in the mid-80s. And by blond, I mean dirty blond. Really dirty. Not Traci Lords in a hot tub dirty. More like swarthy, even though the dude was probably born a day's drive from the Arctic Circle. His skin, too. It had the unhealthy glow of a pink chicken breast breaded in grandma's ashes.

"It doesn't smell like shit," he rasped in a voice simultaneously ghoulish and girlish, like the voice of a Victorian ghost.

Juan parted the drapes and pulled open the patio door. A blast of cool air flushed my lair of its ichorous funk. The sounds of the city, cars and people, streamed in, too. A bird chirped somewhere outside, maybe from the park across the street.

I felt hungry.

Hungry and alive.

I felt hungry enough to return to the fridge, the scene of the crime.

I fished out a piece of cheese and gnawed on it as Svart

and Juan fumigated my room, waving their arms and kicking my discarded clothes into a single pile at the foot of my bed. Svart groaned another "Verdomme" as he firmly shut the door to the bathroom.

The new guy stared at me as I chewed. He stood a bit too close, didn't move as I stepped from the kitchen into the main room. He gazed rapt through faded denim eyes. He kind of sniffed at my neck as I shuffled past him so I could sit on the bed.

"No," he said again in that same rasping voice. "It smells like death, like sickness."

I swallowed my cheese.

"Who the fuck is this guy?"

I mean, I wasn't dead yet.

"I was sick once, as a child, in Malmö." His chest heaved as he inhaled the stale air. "In Sweden."

He inched closer, reached out his hand to touch my cheek.

"Your pallor, it is exquisite. Like a corpse, yet warm. They say you are from a tropical city. Perhaps the corpses there are warm, and they fester immediately."

Svart cut in. This was weird, even by Euro standards.

"This is Nordikron."

Still, it wasn't weird enough to dampen Svart's enthusiasm.

"You remember. Formerly of Astrampsychos. He is a singer phenomenon."

I didn't say anything. Instead, I sat on the bed and fished a pair of socks I'd used last night as gloves out of the covers. I didn't want this guy in my place any longer than necessary.

"And the dried snot on your face … you have the aura, the aroma, even the visage of a plague victim."

I shot a look at Juan, who was about to laugh. People

didn't say shit like this in Miami.

"The snot on my face?" I touched my upper lip and dislodged a dried booger moustache.

"Yeah, thanks for noticing." This was worse than my dad when I was a kid. Sometimes I'd go to hug him goodnight and, instead of hugging me back, he'd kind of wrinkle his nose and ask me, "Have you had a bowel movement today?"

Then this Nordikron guy sat next to me on my bed and started into his own childhood tale.

"In my sickness, as a child, I nearly died."

He leaned back and rested his head against the wall. He had quickly made himself a bit too much at home.

"No, as a point of fact I did die and remain dead. For weeks I languished inside, through the worst part of winter. My nurse wore a mask when she entered my room. She opened the windows, too. It was much worse than this," he gestured at my apartment.

"The stench of death could not be killed by the cold. The stench of death, my frozen fog of dead breath that I saw dissipate into the air, I imagined that these clouds of breath were my soul, a long coil of cloud slowly exiting my body through my mouth, my nose."

I got up and went into the bathroom. Svart was right. Even I thought it smelled bad. Shit streaked the toilet seat. Suspicious brown clumps freckled the floor tiles.

Svart had posted himself over by the patio door, as far away from the bathroom as possible. He flipped through my CD case on the bookshelf, occasionally clucking to himself in disdain.

It's a small apartment though, so I hadn't really escaped Nordikron, who remained on my bed.

"My nurse wiped my face with a warm washcloth," he went on. "She scrubbed and scrubbed, but the stain, the snot, would not come out."

Juan plopped down next to Nordikron.

"You said you died?"

"Yes. And I have the marks to show it. Do you see this mark, this discoloration on my face?"

He poked his pointed nose out like a rat's sniffing snout.

"I have been marked by it since my illness. She tried to scrub it away. She tried to scrub away the scabs that spread from my nostrils to my upper lip, the dried skin that flaked the edges of my mouth."

"Ooh. Yeah, I see it," Juan said. "It's faint, but it's there, like a scar or something."

"One day at dusk, the only lights coming from kerosene lanterns, I stared in the mirror. The inflamed scabs spread from my nostrils to my lower lips, and dried crumbs of skin hung from the edges of my mouth. I realized why she kept scrubbing, this old woman, this peasant."

"A peasant?" Juan asked. He always liked to refer to anybody who wasn't a musician or an artist, anyone who wasn't firmly engaged in some kind of shamanistic vision quest, as a peasant, a sensate beast, a chattel enslaved by base material wants.

"Yes. A peasant. A poor person. Of low class," Nordikron explained as though he hadn't used the right word.

"She was scrubbing at the corpse of the people. The, eh, folk. Scrubbing away at the memory of those that never quite stay buried in the boggy soil. I saw in myself the image of a plague victim, so many who died so suddenly, the swarms of dead from 1349. I had died and my soul had departed. Their souls, still hungry to live, filled my body. In the mirror, I saw the mark of death, the mark of the soul as it leaves the body."

I shut the door, fart fog be damned, and performed my own hasty dermabrasion. As fucked up and creepy as his story was, this guy had hit on something. I looked in the mirror, too. Dark patches underlined each eye. I mean, it seemed worse than the kind you get from not sleeping, partying too hard, and drinking too much. The kind that generally begrimed my visage. The skin wasn't just temporarily discolored, a secondary hangover symptom easily cured with a shower and some coffee. It looked thick and muddy, like dried Silly Putty.

They'll go away, I thought, these patches. Now that I'm not hallucinating about bus routes, now that I'm no longer gripped in fever's freeze. I'll clean the apartment. Eat some vegetables. It will all get better.

I came out of the bathroom. I wanted to get outside, to life, to the sounds of people, cars, movement.

"Come on . . . let's dip," I said, closing the patio door and herding everyone out of the apartment and into the elevator. On the way down, again uncomfortably snuffling at my neck, Nordikron finished his story.

"The mark of death is truth. And beauty. I have learned to distinguish it on others."

The elevator spat us out into a brisk autumn day. We set out at a determined pace. I struggled to keep up. From my apartment, we headed toward the city center.

Svart played the role of the jocular and effusive host. Decked out in camo cargo pants and a Desekration shirt—on the front, that picture of him, corpsepaint clad, wielding some prickly truncheon in front of the now deleafed tree by his place; on the back, a line of his cryptic lyrics: "Winterblast stormforest . . . to winds ov demise"—he marched us through the narrow streets, stopping here and there to point out some bar, the historical significance of some city feature, or the best place to buy Belgian chocolates. He had the zealous energy of a chamber of commerce president eager to court some highly profitable relocating business.

He jocked the singer phenomenon all day long, too. Nordikron's performance on *The Intrapsychic Secret* merited constant celebration and praise, like he'd won a Nobel Prize for Metal Vocal Performance. Like he'd made the hessian *Thriller.*

Svart said things like, "The drum sound . . . crisp and yet like a cavern! How did you achieve this?" or "I must know . . . were your vocals processed at all? Completely inhuman!"

Nordikron, feeding off the fan worship, beamed in his wan, unapproachable way. He regaled us with stories like the one about his near death in Sweden. Or should I say Malmö. I noticed all the stories had a few common elements: each harkened back to that illness, and each took place in some different Eurotown I'd never heard of. As I listened, feeling the cool August breeze on my face, checking out all the different girls and women out on Saturday shopping missions— this one in orange boots, that one, on a bike, with a zebra print scarf trailing in the breeze, I started to perk up even more. I felt thankful that I hadn't been as sick as this guy. Hey, I'd just battled a bit of food poisoning. Some indigestion. Besides, how was I expected to know the ultralimited cooling capacities of my Eurofridge? The same thing could have happened to anybody.

Nordikron, some twenty years after a juvenile bout of fever, seemed to believe that it had actually killed him. Or made him possessed by medieval plague spirits. Or some combination of these things. He constantly alluded to these various theories as if he were trying to figure out what made him such a fucked up little freak. I mean, he was fucked up in a lot of ways. I couldn't even figure out what country he came from. He seemed to be of indeterminate nationality. He was transnational before it was cool. He may have "died" in Sweden, but he didn't say he was a Swede. He didn't say so directly, but I got the impression that his family was loaded, making him the wealthiest nekrocorpse traipsing across Europe. He'd lived in Sweden, Belgium, the Netherlands, at the very least. He jabbered with Svart in Dutch, using that back of the throat monotone that goes hand in hand with the language. Svart seemed even more impressed with him, if that were possible.

"We claim you as one of our own, a true Gentenaar! True, your time in Limberg has given you some of that dialect, but no non-native could speak so well."

When Juan asked him about all the languages he knew, he kind of smirked.

"The languages, they are not that different," he said. "They have the same historic grammar. They are the voice of one body. If you can read Swedish, you can probably read Nederlands; if you can read Nederlands, it is not so hard to read English."

As we stood on Sint Michielsbrug, an old bridge adorned with a statue of St. Michael dispatching a serpent, we looked at rows of restaurants lining the waterfront of the Graslei. Tourboats shuttled down the Leie River. Svart named off the trio of towers poking up beyond: Sint Baafskathedraal, the Belfort Tower, Sint Niklaaskirk. Svart beamed. It was the complete opposite of the tortured expression on his shirt.

"A well-known history professor at Oxford," he looked at Juan and I knowingly, as though we should feel some surge of pride for this prof because he, too, was an English speaker, "who has been to many of the best European cities saw this sight and declared it the most medieval landscape in all Europe."

As we crossed the bridge and moved toward the towers, he pointed out the Gulden Draak, that giant sculpture at the top of the Belfort Tower. The one Juan had drawn on his demo tape.

"That is the Gulden Draak. Its snout points toward Brugge. We erected it in 1377 to stave off their cowardly attacks. It has proved an effective deterrent."

The Svart tour included entrance to this tower, too. He sprung for tickets, though, as he haggled with the guy in the kiosk at the base of the Belfort, it was clear he had free passes because of his mom's membership in some local historical society.

We trudged up countless steps, ascending in a winding spiral. If it weren't for the electric lights set every ten steps or so apart, I'd say we were going back in time. The grit of the stones held the scars of centuries. After my week of sickness and solitude, I felt a bit woozy. I could see why this was a key stop on the Svart tour, though. Juan and Nordikron loved it. They raced up the steps together. Juan paused under each lamp and posed dramatically. The yellow sulfur glare cast Haunted Mansion shadows across his face.

I wanted to ask Svart how many more steps there were, but he'd already disappeared in the darkness and around the bend. Above, I heard the creak of a heavy door, followed by the thud of footsteps on a wooden floor. I was getting close. A noise, the screech of rusty door hinges, welled into a loud whine, like a buzz saw, or something even louder, a rampaging helicopter. The lights snapped off. I grabbed the handrail to brace myself. The slightest pinprick of daylight streamed down from the open door. The tower, a serpentine echo chamber, magnified the sound, which continued, unabated, like a fire alarm you can't turn off—was this part of the tour?—then modulated into a word, "through," but drawn out and tortured, a giant's death rattle or a seismic shudder.

Nordikron, displaying his talents.

Without a pause, the rest of the message followed, flooding the stairway with the voice of one creepy little dude: "Through me the way into the suffering city." To get the full effect, try to spend about ten seconds on each syllable. "Thhhruuuuuuwwww" or, for full diacritical accuracy, "Thhhrüüüüüüwwww." Maybe he was dead, like he said, because no one living could produce those noises, so loud, so long, so impossibly sepulchral, without taking a breath. The hairs on my neck and arms pulsed like a thousand-needled Peak Program Meter. The door slammed shut with a massive timpani thud followed by muffled laughter.

"Singer phenomenon" without a doubt, I thought as I fumbled up the steps.

I pushed open the heavy door, expecting to join my bandmates, but they weren't there. Instead, a dragon's head stared at me. Its curled bronze tongue practically lapped deez nuts. They'd replaced the first, this medieval draak, in the nineteenth century and stuck it up here. I guess they didn't want a rusted metal reptile crashing down on passers-by. Parts of its skin, oxidized green, had been peeled away to show its curved wooden frame. It resembled the opaque cicada shells you find glued to Florida trees in late summer. A supersized metal exoskeleton.

Some exhibition cases showing how they made the current model filled the rest of the room. I heard Juan squeal in delight from a doorway leading out to a viewing platform overlooking the city. I headed out there and took in the city, a steepled labyrinth far below. Sure, you could see some roads in the distance, some cars parked here and there, and, if you looked really hard, you could make out the railway station, but other than that, this view probably hadn't changed much since the spirits possessing Nordikron last culled beets from the loamy soil. We peered over peaked orange roofs that jutted out at a cacophony of angles. The crooked rooflines overlapped like the fractured planes of a Braque still life.

Juan bounced back and forth along the walkway. He held a tiny black and gold telescope, more like the kind you'd blow your allowance on at a museum exhibit on Blackbeard than anything actually intended for astral observation. He stretched out of the window opening and pointed his telescope up.

If you ignored the little sign telling you not to do what he was doing, you could see the veined wings, the blimpish belly, of the Gulden Draak framed by the pale blue sky. With a telescope like Juan's, you'd get a slightly magnified view of the scene.

Standing next to Juan, Nordikron pulled a cassette recorder, the kind reporters used to use, with tiny microcassettes, out of his back pocket. He held it to his lips and recorded himself saying, "The dragon, that old serpent, which is the devil, and Satan." He played the recording back a few times, his ear mashed against the speaker. He recorded a few versions, too, each time saying the words a little bit differently.

"Up here, it's like some gilded cloud," Juan marveled.

A gilded cloud ready to crash.

13.
Stoverij met Frietjes

Sights seen, it was time to talk business. I hadn't really had to talk all day; I just moved along, pulling up the rear. There hadn't even been any awkward silences in need of filling, no long minutes of dull mutual staring that, in my experience, were par for the course with these northern types. Svart promised a good meal at a restaurant he'd gone to for years. He saw the brief look of fright cross my face when he mentioned food.

He smiled, said "Don't worry, kiddo. We take care of you good," and tousled my hair.

The restaurant was tucked off a small side street across from one of Gent's many city squares. Long wooden windowboxes holding forests of ivy and herbs flanked the front doors. As we stood at the entrance, a street car, packed with shoppers, rumbled down the street. An entire week had passed, shoppers and workers shuffled about the town day and night, and me, for that whole time, trapped by sickness, stuck in my own track shuttling between class, toilet, bed.

Svart held open the door of the restaurant and we all filed into its rustic and cozy interior. With its high wood beamed ceilings and long tables flanked by oak benches, it felt like a ski lodge, or the kind of place you'd see in an L.L. Bean catalog.

Juan sat next to me and pulled a sketchbook out of his satchel. Nordikron's cape got stuck as he settled into the chair across from me. The child safety enclosure emitted a tiny Velcro growl as it strained against his neck.

"Where's Tomi?" I asked.

"At the gym," Svart said, then waved the waiter to the table.

"Vier pots Primus, alstublieft."

Nordikron put his hand on Svart's arm.

"No . . . my voice. I do not drink alcohol."

Svart grimaced. If Juan or I had turned down a drink—even me, my face as gray and pale as the slate tiles of the plaza we'd walked across to get to the restaurant, my stomach a fetid bacteria fishbowl of Glucozade, he would have questioned our manhood, cursed at us in an incomprehensible low country slur. Juan stopped doodling and looked at me; you could tell he was thinking the same thing.

"I prefer warm tea. Chamomile, preferably. With honey."

Svart ordered the tea, then regained his composure. He said, in his most cheerful voice, "We will enjoy true Belgische gerechten, regional specialties." He then murmured the order in that low mumble Belgians associate with mannerly politeness. As the waiter turned from the table, Nordikron touched his elbow, and muttered something equally incomprehensible. The waiter nodded, then trotted off to the kitchen.

The drinks came out, three huge beers in glasses that looked like barrels with handles, and one dainty cup of tea. The word "pot" Svart had used to order proved an accurate descriptor. As Nordikron fussed over his tea, mixing honey and milk into it like he was preparing some elixir suitable for

Goat Song Sacrifice

Santa's elves, Svart looked at Juan and I with something I could only describe as warmth. Sure, we hadn't made *The Intrapsychic Secret*. Sure, he'd never dare to stock any of the music we'd made in his elitist shop, and, unlike Nordikron, we lacked pan-European upbringings, but at least we could drink beer, like, I'm sure you're thinking, true heavy metallers. I wondered if my innards were up to the task. This far into our relationship, I already knew Nordikron and I would never agree on much, but tea sounded good. Or carrot juice.

As Nordikron stirred his tea, he said, "I saw your keyboard."

He listed the exact model number then asked, "Are you composing anything for our project, for *Infernö*?"

Svart sniggered. Before I could answer, he cut me off and said, "I told him already to get rid of that thing."

Then he launched into the stump speech he'd been giving me all summer. You know, keyboards are for Hall and Oates, not black metal. Downtuned does not mean evil. Any form of musical expression not hashed out on the first two Bathory albums was to be regarded as unseemly noise not made by real men.

"That's unfortunate. Is it for sale then?" He turned to Svart and added, "I'm not a real man. I'm dead."

I told him he could have it for a hundred bucks.

"Oh, it's worth more than that," he said. "I'll take it off your hands."

Svart realized this band meeting wasn't working out how he'd imagined. If I objected to one of his musical pronouncements, he'd just tell me I didn't know what I was talking about. But Nordikron? To him, Svart was just some third rate disciple.

To put a more positive spin on his commandments, Svart abandoned his string of "thou shalt nots." He described his vision of a masterwork that fused the grim atmosphere of Hellhammer's *Apocalyptic Raids* with the thrash perfection of Kreator's *Coma of Souls*. All topped, of course, with Nordikron's pinnacle vocals.

Nordikron absently patted his cape during the diatribe. He produced a small glass vial from somewhere within, from some concealed pocket sized just right for a Nerf batarang. It was a brown vial with a black cap. When I was a kid, I used to find similar ones in the gutters on the edges of the streets that bordered the mangrove swamp. For "medicine." Instead of white crystals, this one was filled with some dark fluid.

At one point, Svart laughed, then reached for Nordikron's shoulder. Nordikron flinched out of his grasp and nearly dropped the vial. His spider fingers shook as he settled it safely onto the table.

"These are only ideas," Svart said. "It does not matter. What matters is you have joined our band."

He raised a toast.

"You have joined Desekration!"

Juan and I hoisted our mugs. We held them there for a long awkward moment until Nordikron, very unwillingly, clinked them with his flowered cup.

Soon, the food came: three steaming platters of beef stew, an enormous basket of friets, and, for Nordikron, a salad served on a green, leaf-shaped plate. The stew, thick chunks of meat steeped in a hearty brown gravy equal parts flour and burgundy wine, sprigs of parsley strewn across the top, settled my stomach with the first bite. The mixture of stew— "Gentse stoverij" is what Svart called it—with fries and beer quelled any salmonella splinter cells bunkered down inside.

As we gorged, Nordikron nibbled at his salad. He held his silverware stiffly, his bony index fingers deftly gliding the handle, the blade, cutting each piece of lettuce, slice of carrot, wedge of tomato, into tiny pieces. Svart, by contrast, dunked the friets—wide cut and oily—into the brown gravy in pairs, then folded them into his mouth.

Between bouts of chewing, Svart laid out his grand ambitions for writing and recording the masterwork. He revealed that he'd talked to Nekrokor since I'd moved out. Since Nordikron had lent us his talents. He made it clear that Nekrokor endorsed Desekration. He made it clear that Nekrokor eagerly awaited the completed *Infernö* master tapes. He made it clear that Nekrokor wanted *Infernö* to be the next sonic plague unleashed on the world by Despondent Abyss.

"He said it will be a pesticide against Christianity!" Svart added triumphantly.

He made it clear that Nekrokor would help to fund it all, too. I perked up. Money. That hadn't been part of my initial contract discussions with the guy. Finally, he made it especially clear that the Desekration juggernaut had overtaken Katabasis. It had consumed Katabasis with the same unavoidable force of Unicron swallowing some insignificant moon or, for that matter, Svart himself choking down another handful of friets.

Nordikron, his salad finished except for a fleck or two of corn here, an untouched crouton there, set his fork and knife down with a tinkle of metal on porcelain that somehow overpowered everything Svart had to say. Even the stuff about money.

"I have no intention of lending my talent to a cover band."

Svart blanched, "What do you mean? We're no cover band. We've discussed how this will work, you and I."

"I hear you talking about music like it is a toy—a fun little kit that can be snapped together like so or like so. Riffs from here, mood from there. That misses the point of what we are doing. Of what I intend to do by working with you. That is the way of trends, this mixed with that. It is neither pure nor true."

He took his fork and jabbed it in Juan's plate. He held up a stew bit impaled on its tines.

"Music and food go together, don't they? The best food is pure. And they both nourish the spirit."

He pointed the fork, the meat, at me.

"Food transforms," he said. "You know that especially well, I am sure. That lesson is, shall we say, fresh on your mind. It is like this meat you all have gobbled mindlessly. You have inadvertently swallowed the lives of animals slaughtered for this purpose. In the last twitch of their death, their muscles swelled with the toxins of their fear. You have eaten their fear, making you prone to that emotion. That emotion sways your faculties and you live as animals. As beasts raised for the slaughter. As sheep among wolves."

Svart huffed, reached for a friet, then stopped himself.

"You have fed on fear, which is weakness. The flesh you have eaten becomes your flesh. Someday, through Pythagorean transmutation, your flesh will become a nourishing stew for worms."

He plunked the fork back into Juan's dish.

"And speaking of worms and meat, friend, you should watch where you wriggle your stew bit."

He sighed, then lifted his little vial. The gloopy fluid churned inside.

"My protein is given willingly. With pleasure, even."

With that, he twisted off the cap and drank, making snuffling noises as the liquid glopped down into his tongue-waggling mouth.

"You three are clueless, but I will work with you. Nekrokor has played me your practice tapes. You, Svart, have enthusiasm, but lack direction. You, Juan, have imagination, but lack skill. And you? I cannot call you 'David.' It is too Hebraic. I thought you not serious enough until I saw you. The fever has lifted, but left its mark. You know what I mean—the mark of the Devil sits heavily on you. Perhaps there is hope."

I left the restaurant alone. We'd agreed to meet for practice later in the week. None of us had really known how to respond to what Nordikron said. It was evident he was in control. Svart didn't even finish his stew.

The arrangement Svart had made with Nekrokor was clear: if Nordikron joined the band, we'd get money to make the album. We all wanted this. Nordikron might even have wanted this, too. But I don't think any of us—not even Svart—realized how challenging it would be to work with the guy. It would be work, that was certain. Still, it wasn't like he'd make us clock in. We weren't exactly employees.

Walking home, reveling in my good health, my full stomach, I thought, it was worth it to live in this city. The cold, paired with the white lights illuminating the city square I walked down—its turn of the century gazebo, its straight row of bushes—felt clean, heavenly even. The city square, its flagstones scrubbed daily by a giant streetsweeper, could be heaven on a night like tonight. My stomach felt like this square: bright, airy, scrubbed clean. After a week of slime and shit, my anus probably gleamed like marble.

In good spirits, I sprinted up the stairs to my apartment. Then I stopped, my key in the lock, and noticed something I hadn't seen before. A brown streak, finger width, stretched across the top of the doorframe.

It wasn't stoverij.

14.
Death Metal
Is Not the Metal of Death

The bags under my eyes stuck around for a while. Long after I scrubbed the dried blood off my doorframe. The gray crescents beneath each eye. They reminded me of the very beginnings of a pothole, the slightest depression that widened, bit by bit, until it opened up to swallow your foot, your bicycle tire, all of you into the earth. That's what I thought one night when I swerved on my bike to miss one such giant pock mark as I thudded down a cobblestoned hill by Overpoortstraat. My bike. I'd just rented a bike, one of the taxi yellow ones that the hordes of foreign students used to get around town. I hadn't ridden one since middle school, so my technique, especially downhill on potholed cobblestones, was sketchy and erratic.

Ahead, Tomi careened down the hill. The distance between our bikes widened by the second. While I gripped the handbrake and inched down the hill with a metallic squeal, Tomi passed other bikers, even cars, with steely determination.

Goat Song Sacrifice

He still didn't say much. At practices, he'd show up, disappear behind the drum kit, then batter away like an atomic metronome until we were done. But if you brought up anything to do with exercise, the outdoors, any kind of physical activity, what Europeans call "sport," he'd open up. He'd talk. He'd give you tips on the best places to hike, the location of a free indoor pool, a good store for camping supplies.

And the best place to rent a bike. When I asked him where he got his, it was like he became another person. He perked up. He spoke in sentences, not just single words. He immediately volunteered to take me to the rental place. He hustled us out of practice so that we'd make it before the place closed. As we walked over, he told me about the features of the bike he'd rented and why it was so good: it came with two locks to stave off thieves, it had a handbrake and rear caliper brakes, and this place would replace any part that broke, no extra charge. He'd already snapped a chain on an uphill and had it fixed within an hour.

After I got the bike, he invited me to go with him to the movies. He was supposed to meet his wife, Liza, and one of her friends at the multiplex down the hill from Overpoortstraat to see some Hollywood action film. In English with Dutch subtitles. I said I'd go.

The two girls stood in front of the movie theater. One of them resembled a prepubescent Ellen in the grip of New Wave nostalgia. She had spiky blond hair and translucent purple glasses. The lenses and the frames were purple. Tomi stood a foot or so away from her and they both leaned forward to exchange the slightest peck, more like two penguins lightly tapping beaks than newlyweds on a date.

I thought at first that the other girl had to be Tomi's. She was a rocker chick. She wasn't just a rocker chick. She was a metalhead. She had on tight black jeans, a spiked belt, and a

111

weathered Ostrogoth shirt. Ostrogoth—I don't expect you to know that one. I didn't, though I pretended I did. When I met up with Svart the next day, I asked him. In the '80s, they were like Belgium's less commercial, less talented, less refined answer to the Scorpions. The shirt she wore even had a metal scorpion on it, each airbrushed claw cupping one of her breasts. She had dyed black hair, silver hoop earrings, and dark brown eyes. To top it all off, she also had deep bruised craters beneath each eye. Like me. She was either severely hungover, sick, or, if Nordikron's theories are to be believed, marked as the Devil's own.

She smelled like wet cigarette butts, too. I got her number, no problem.

At the next practice, Tomi said, "Maria"—that's the Ostrogoth—"she said she likes you."

I hadn't called her yet. According to the primeval calculations of mantime, I still had a day or so left. I was still within my 72-hour waiting period. But I knew I would. The time to idly collect phone numbers had passed. Maybe it was the way the spiked belt gripped her hips, or the fact that I had never heard of Ostrogoth, or just a fog of pheromones, tobacco, and stale beer filtered through the thin gauze of her ancient shirt, but I thought I was ready to get past Natasha. To leap into the breach. With pike bent bravely. Besides, I'd nearly run out of hand lotion.

Message relayed, Tomi went back to adjusting a cymbal and didn't speak to me again that night. He didn't need to; we saw each other all the time. That fall, it felt like we were always crammed in our practice room at the Begijnhof. We had that easy familiarity I used to have with the other losers who worked with me at Booksalot.

Goat Song Sacrifice

We practiced a few times a week. Nordikron insisted. It was a period of practice and growth for the band. Loathing, too. Familiarity breeds contempt, right?

Most people think if you're in a band, you play with the other members. But you also play against them. Or despite them.

Sometimes you play to get away from them. That's how I approached it. So I didn't have to spend too much time with Nordikron. With Mathias. A few practices in, he deigned to use his real name with us. I think it's because I kept harassing him about how loud he had his amp. The slightest whisper, or breath, or dog slobbering about Satan's coming millennium, overpowered the rest of us. Like he wanted to be Bono or something. A little Nekrobono. With the vocals ten times louder than any of the instruments.

A few practices in and I'd had enough. I couldn't ignore the fact that I couldn't hear my part. Or anyone else's.

I tried to be polite at first. As a general rule, you should keep anyone who drinks blood, but not beer, at arm's length.

I asked, "Hey, Nordikron. Can you turn it down?"

No response. I asked a few more times without success.

"Fucking dick," I hissed, then tried again. "Hey, Nordikron. I need to hear what I'm playing."

He ignored me.

"Hey, Nordikron. Nordikron. Nordikron."

Each time I said it, I emphasized that middle syllable just a bit more.

Dick. Dick. Dick.

Nor-dick-ron.

Finally, I just screamed, "Hey, uh, Dick-ron, this isn't a fucking poetry slam," turned my amp as high as it would go, then pressed my guitar against it, the distortion rising in an overpowering squeal.

Everyone stopped playing. He put down his mic and stepped over to me.

He said, "I'm sorry. I did not hear you. I was completely taken over. By the dead. You can call me Mathias. That will break the spell."

Svart didn't like me harassing his singer phenomenon.

"That's out of order, David," he said.

But he did like the permission to call the guy by his real name.

"Show Mathias some respect."

Which was exactly what he didn't show to Juan. Any respect. I was used to these kinds of flare ups and petty arguments during practices—in Valhalla, John and Phil always argued between songs, one of them spitting in the other one's Mountain Dew to show his disapproval, the other one dumping his own guitar in the trash can, then storming out of the room. I'd spared Juan that kind of treatment in our Katabasis days. Maybe I'd spoiled him?

We got back to playing. Mathias kept his soul vomiting at a respectable level.

In the first few weeks with him, we managed to turn every riff that Svart and I had dicked around with over the summer into complete songs. They all sounded darker, more sinister, with our secret weapon, the mouth of the abyss. Even "Winterminion Ensorcels."

It's just that Juan couldn't really keep pace with the band's sharpened aggression. He stood in the corner and leaned against the walls. Sweat dripped down his face. He'd undone the row of pearl buttons on the front of his Victorian smock. His pinstriped blazer lay in a heap on the floor.

Svart loomed over Juan. His bass hung from his neck like some massive anvil. He clapped his hands along with Tomi's tumult of beats. Juan echoed a few notes behind everyone else. Every few measures he skipped a few notes to catch up.

"Come on, little man," Svart said.

He thumped his bass, starting at Juan's pace, then quickly catching up to the rest of us.

"You play like this, but we need ..." Svart's hand blurred with motion.

The practice room shook with a vibrating tonal barrage.

Juan got to about three notes for every four of Svart's, a notable improvement, with Svart shouting "faster ... faster ... move your pick!" into his face like a drill instructor the whole time.

When Juan finally caught up, Svart grunted, then moved back to his usual position over by Nordikron.

"It must be nekro!" he yelled.

Nordikron twisted his body like a demonic Gumby: "Ne-chrauwww."

After practice, Svart continued his pep talk with Juan.

"When you keep up, you're pretty good," he said. "Good tone. Eerie."

"Just remember though. This isn't sloppy seconds," he slapped Juan's back. "You know what I mean? This is *Infernö* we are making here. That death metal you used to play, that won't cut it."

"He's right," Mathias said. "Death metal is not the metal of death."

15.
Manifestations of the Beast
in Flesh

When I got back to the building, I checked my mail. This compulsive habit rarely yielded results. My parents sent cards that arrived exactly on whatever holiday—major or minor—was in question. Sometimes with money. Last month, they'd sent me a Labor Day card. No message. Just "Mom and Dad" written on the inside. Just their names. Titles, really. And no money.

I pulled out a postcard, but I knew it couldn't be from them. We were in the long holiday-free zone that stretched until Halloween. The postcard was just a photo glued to an index card. Its frayed edges, combined with a white gash through the photo paper, suggested my mailbox was the end of a long, perilous journey.

On an October evening, under the dim lobby lights, the picture was like a portal to another world, a snapshot of a sylvan world, a sun drenched tree with winding roots. My heart pounded faster than Tomi's most protein-shake-fueled blizzard beat. I recognized the tree. A ficus tree in Merrie

Goat Song Sacrifice

Christmas Park. I flipped the card over and saw her signature, Natasha, at the end of a typed message:

> *You're hard to find out there in the wide world. Do you remember me? I am a quiet girl, a gentle spirit, who offers you peace. Even if we never see each other again, know that you can find peace. You only have to look.*

I puzzled over the message. Cryptic. The final send off or an invitation back? I couldn't tell. I still can't. I stepped in the elevator, mashed the button for my floor, and tried to take in every detail of the picture. The living tree, the all-enveloping sun. More importantly, I wanted to absorb every detail of the shadow imposed on the trunk of the tree. Natasha's shadow. The edges of her long shadow skirt, the slightest trace of a shadow breast, the shadowy knot of her hair in a bun. The shadow of a camera in her shadowed hands. She took this picture. Alone. A solitary shadow. Self-portrait with ficus. She took it and not that guy I'd seen her with before I left Miami. The cool guy with his hand on her back.

Once upstairs, I cracked a beer and sat on the bed. I fingered the edges of the card, the flaps where she hadn't completely glued the photo down. I found the end of a hair and pulled it out. A single hair, long and dark. I balled it up in my palm and held it to my nose. Beneath the eau de Elmers, there was the faintest note of jasmine, the perfume she wore.

I didn't know whether or not to write her back. I wanted to. I missed her. So I picked up a postcard at the newsstand by the grocery store—it had a plate of waffles or something—and carried it around for a few days. There wasn't much space to fill, but I didn't know what to say. I didn't know how to respond. I mean, there's the truth, right, but that may have been too true:

> *I remember you. I'm obsessed by you. Haunted by you. My guilt is a thick shroud and I can't wriggle free. I think about you as soon as I wake up. Every morning. Before I take a piss, even. Belgium is great—waffles and black metal!*

At the next practice, I sat in the Begijnhof's common area and waited for the rest of the band. The postcard, blank side up, rested on the table. Slowly, a message came to me through the muffled sounds of piano lessons and jazz quartets in other practice rooms. I wrote it down: "Hey Natasha! Thank you for the card. Things here are good."

That's all I'd written. I was just about to add the last masterful line—either "I hope to hear from you soon," which I thought was maybe pushing it and basically the same thing as "I think about you as soon as I wake up," or the less revealing option, "I hope things are good with you"—when Mathias came through the door.

"Ah, a postcard to send back home. Is it to your parents? I'm sure they'll proudly display it in their trailer."

"It's not for my parents," I said. I wished Svart would show up soon; he had the key to the practice room. "They don't live in a trailer."

He hovered over me, reading the card over my shoulder.

I covered it with my hand.

"Left handed, eh? I am, too."

Then, he went and opened the practice room. I guess Svart had given him a key. I went back to my card. I finished it off with "I hope to hear from you soon." It was the truth.

After practice, I slid the postcard into a mailbox.

Goat Song Sacrifice

I noticed the wart about a week later. Warts, I mean. Plural. At their greatest range, they formed a bumpy wartscape that nearly circled the ring finger of my left hand. Because of a guitar solo. I came into practice with something good, a line of notes I'd been humming to myself for a few days. Svart generally disavowed any solos. Especially for me. But I'd trimmed my playing of its death metal excesses. I knew, by instinct, that anything remotely train-like in its sound, any rhythmic chug-a-chug-ing, would lead to a stern glare, a rebuke, then a temporary exile from the practice space while I went to the bathroom to listen to a song of his choice—"Return of the Darkness and Evil" was the last one he'd punished me with—on a crappy boombox. I wouldn't be allowed back into the practice room until I played enough of it back to him to convince him that its inspired tones had sufficiently cleansed my consciousness.

I felt the wart when I played the solo. Its crusted edges brushed against my middle knuckle as I stretched for the highest notes. As I ran up the scale, its sandpapery surface rubbed my skin in time with the beat. I cut the solo short—which Svart liked—then stuck to power chords. But even then, you use your ring finger. It can't rub your middle finger because that one's out of the way, but every time I looked down at my hand, the craggy dome of that most imposing wart—the Everest of its cauliflower range—glared back at me.

Between songs, we took a break. I made the mistake of inspecting my finger too closely. Mathias noticed immediately. He diagnosed my malady while I still tried to convince myself it was a clogged pore, a temporary mole, a minor skin imperfection I must have always had, but only now noticed

119

because the months of sun deprivation had produced a pale-ness my skin had never before known. A little sun would shrink that thing, I thought. Just a tiny bubble symptomatic of a vitamin D deficiency. An hour spent sitting in the sun with a magnifying glass and I'd scorch that fucker away. Melt it down, no problem.

Mathias wasn't so easily deluded.

"Ah, the Devil has graced you with another mark," he said. "You've nearly collected them all. The shadows beneath your eyes. Left handed. Now, as an extra sign of diabolic grace, a supernumerary nipple. On your left hand. The ring finger, even. A Satanic diamond marking you as His."

He set the mic on the floor and took my hand. He cradled it in his hands. He even poked and prodded the offending wart with his own fingers. He bent his mouth close, like he intended to kiss it or, worse, lick it. That's what they're for, right? Supernumerary nipples? I pulled my hand away, shoved it in my pocket, and grimaced as the wart crust scraped the denim on its way in.

Mathias couldn't have picked a more conspicuous mo-ment to notice it. He said that stuff about the Devil's signs directly into the mic. Svart, of course, bounded over. Juan and Tomi followed soon after.

"Verdomme, look at that thing!" Svart bellowed. "It's massive."

Juan and Tomi stared at the spectacle, too. Each offered their respective folk remedies:

"My mom always rubs a banana peel on hers."

"Urinate on it. Before showering. That worked for my brother."

The next morning, I stopped at the Apotheek on my way to

class. I held out my hand to the pharmacist like some Stepford wife displaying a massive rock. The pharmacist sent me away with a bottle of salicylic acid and a box of fuzzy oval patches. I diligently started my treatment regimen in the school bathroom during the morning break, but didn't have much success.

That night at practice, Mathias tut-tutted my medicated and bandaged finger, saying, "You can try, but you can never erase the Devil's mark."

I wish I could say he was wrong but on this, at least, he spoke the truth. So, from here on out, just imagine me with one of the following on my finger: a tidy beige wart rug covering a dense application of salicylic acid solution, a blistered and oozing sore, or the beginnings of a resurrected wart rising through the slime of what was recently a blistered and oozing sore. A wingless wart phoenix in its cycle of birth and rebirth.

"You're not the only one with that particular mark," Mathias said. "Nekrokor has one, too. I'm surprised you have not noticed it. It resembles an eye in his palm. It's bigger than yours. Almost like a volcano, since he always picks out the center. He has been prescribed this same medicine. Salicylic acid. It forms a burning paste. When mixed with a few other items, it holds up quite well in the post, don't you think?"

He knew about my first contact with Nekrokor, the letter. May warts encrust your playing fingers. So shall it be.

Mathias continued, "He tests it on his arms. He says he likes the burn. Every sadist needs a masochist. He's long given up on trying to get rid of it. Rather, he lets it grow, cuts it off, and then sends its pieces, embedded in the salve, to offending parties. Sometimes, he just burns it out of his palm with a cigarette."

Embedded in the salve. So his curse had worked. But that

had been months ago. And these had just come to life. Still, I thought, a curse through mail could be the right explanation. I mean, Natasha thought of herself as a witch. She was always reading some arcane book about the goddess, the mystical wisdom of femininity, stuff I didn't pay too much attention to, being generally more interested in getting her out of her clothes. Or thinking of her as, like, the sexy witch. Drawing down the moon in a pointy hat and nothing else, she enacts a ritual that culminates in a spirited broom ride.

When you think of warts, you think of the unsexy witches. You think of the crusty bump at the end of some crone's schnoz. It jaggles to and fro as she cackles at your misfortune.

By this time, Svart came over to shepherd me back to my guitar.

"The explanation is simple," he said. "This guy, he jacks off too much. At least, that's what my mom thinks."

Maria didn't notice it. The wart. Or she didn't care. One Friday, we met at one of my favorite bars. The Dulle Griet. Juan and I just called it the shoe bar. They had this giant glass that looked like a long funnel fused with a light bulb. Better suited for lab experiments than beer drinking. It came with a wooden stand to keep it upright. Anyway, they wouldn't let you use the glass unless you gave them one of your shoes. Then, the bar guy put your shoe in a basket and raised it to the ceiling. To keep people from stealing the crazy glass. You got your shoe back when you were done.

I liked the shoe beer. That's nearly a liter of liquid. But the real reason I'd go there is for their bier van de maand offer. Beer of the month. Buy one get one free. Europe is relatively devoid of these kinds of deals. Juan and I went there because it reminded us of home.

Goat Song Sacrifice

I met Maria outside of the bar. Maybe that's why I took her there? The certainty of a discount bargain made me less nervous. She still had on the Ostrogoth shirt. Same jeans and spiked belt. She had on a leather jacket, too. We sat outside and drank. Over the span of a few hours, two for one turned into ten for five. When we got up to leave, Maria held onto my arm and I held onto the wicker chair while I flicked a few coins onto the table.

We stumbled out toward the city center. The brightly lit buildings, ancient and unchanging, against the black backdrop of a cloudless night can make anything romantic. Even the drunken hook up of two dirtbags. So when I put my arm around her waist, fastened my thumb between the belt and her jeans, and asked "Where should we go now?" we both already knew the answer.

"Your place," she said. "And I know what we'll do there."

My balls stirred; they detected a call to action. Part of me, though, thought of that postcard. Natasha's shadow. Why had I written "I hope to hear from you soon" if I was just going to betray her again?

Maria must have sensed some kind of hesitation from me. She held my shoulders and gave me a cockeyed grin.

"But first," she said, "I want you to kiss me."

She stretched up to me—she wasn't tall. I didn't move, but I looked around wildly—for an escape, for some kind of divine sign, for permission, I don't know what. A tram turned the corner and glided past with a nearly silent whoosh, just as Maria bit my lower lip and sucked it into her mouth. On the tram, some girl, Natasha's doppelgänger sent to track my every move, stared out at us, her hair smooshed against the window like a crushed spider.

Eventually, I kissed Maria back. I savored her wet charcoal tongue. We went to my apartment, lip locked the entire way. As soon as we made it in, she asked if I had any condoms.

I slipped into the bathroom where a lone condom lay in the medicine chest next to the dental floss. Lay. I'm going to get laid, I thought.

It took less than ten seconds to get it—I sensed that time was of the essence—but in that time, she'd fully prepared for action.

She was on her hands and knees, naked except for a black thong. And a necklace. An inverted cross hung between her breasts from a silver chain. She faced the wall like a dog nosing up to the front door, leash in its jaws, and aching for a walksie. Like a dog. On her knees. Doggie style.

I climbed on the bed, scooting over the sheets on my knees until I was behind her. Then, I rolled her panties over her ass and down her thighs. My fingers squeezed her meaty haunches and I pushed myself in. My dick sank like a butter knife into a jumbo jar of mayonnaise. One you'd left out on the counter for a while. Warm and goopy.

At the end, she let loose a wild Chewbacca bark.

16.
The Goat Song

It wasn't all warts and jack off jokes that fall. Slowly, Mathias shaped the band and took control. Svart's *Infernö* became Nordikron's *Infernö*. Svart's songs—the ones we'd pieced together over the summer—became Nordikron's songs.

And when I say Nordikron, I mean someone quite different from Mathias. Mathias was the guy who showed up to practice absently strewing the floor with receipts, tram tickets, and other bits of paper, each scrap marked with a phrase, a word, some occult glyph. Nordikron was the presence that brought those scraps, those words, to life. If I switch between the two, it's because he switched between them, too. The more time I spent with him, the more I could make out the jagged edge between them. I think Mathias wanted to be Nordikron all the time, but no one—living, dead, or undead—has the energy to pull that off.

By the time he told us he'd set up our first gig, he was in control. It was like he'd been the one who assembled us all, not Svart. Like he'd come up with the band name. I started to feel as though the whole idea of the album, this gritty discordant thing, had all come from Nordikron's warped mind.

He dotted *Infernö*'s umlauted "o."

The day that Mathias told us about the show, things shifted a bit. Svart's aggressive tutoring came to a halt. Svart never punished me with Bathory songs again. He no longer boxed Juan into the corner, or critiqued his playing.

Practice that day was like any other. We met in the Begijnhof in the evening. I'd spent the day studying Dutch. The niveau een final exam was only a couple of weeks away. Helena had passed out a review sheet that morning and as I looked it over, it dawned on me that I might actually pass.

We knew we were ready to send a rough mix of completed tracks to the label. We didn't have enough songs for an album, but Svart wanted us to send some of the stuff we'd been doing since Nordikron joined.

We'd already taped a demo version of "Winterminion Ensorcels," but that day Nordikron announced we were going to do it again.

"I listened to the tape, and that song is the weakest," he said. He pulled his lyric sheets out of his satchel with the authority of your hardest teacher about to start class.

Svart looked down sheepishly at his bread loaf hands. It was basically his song, after all.

"The weakness lies in the refrain."

You know the part. It's where he spits out the words "winterminion ensorcels" in a logorrheic explosion.

Then, he shamed Svart a little bit more.

"I am giving voice to the obliteration of the soul. What you want me to do, Jurgen, is not that. It is the opposite of that. It is naming a song through simple repetition. This is the material you had before I arrived and I respect that. But I have added my own interpretation as well."

That's how he talked about his singing, his vokills, whatever you want to call it. He saw himself interpreting. Not words or ideas, but the experience of death.

After he put a blank tape in the console, he pulled his little microrecorder out of his messenger bag. Then he motioned for us to start the song. He got to the refrain, to that repetition designed to destroy lungs wrought of living flesh. Nordikron hammered it out with extra verve, as if to show Svart that his critique had nothing to do with the limits of his singing. As he did, he held the tape recorder up to the mic and pressed play. His voice wailed through the line in a single take that evoked the sound of brittle fingers slowly tearing a photograph in two. The two approaches, the fast and the slow, the intelligible and the elemental, words and vocalized sound, merged together. The crappy hiss from the tape recorder added that nekro atmosphere Svart had been yammering on about for weeks.

At the end of practice, Mathias popped his tape out of the console. He'd run us through multiple takes of our songs, and supplemented his singing with the hand-held recorder in each one.

"I will make sure that this gets to Nekrokor," he said. "You should know that we will open for his band, for Astrampsychos, the first Friday in November. The show will be here, in Gent, at the Frontline."

The Frontline was a tiny club off Overpoortstraat, not too far from Svart's favorite kebab spot. Even though it was small, a lot of bands coming through Belgium played there.

We all waited for his next command. I think we were all surprised by his announcement, and how he mentioned it so nonchalantly at the end of practice. We had about two weeks to prepare. If Svart had lined up something like that, he'd have made sure we knew about it as soon as possible.

"Astrampsychos," Mathias mused as he shoved the tape into his bag. "They should really change that name. I'm the one who came up with it. And they kicked me out."

Juan asked, "Isn't that some kind of Greek name? It means 'starry mind,' right?"

"Our Latin is a linguist, I see. The name of an ancient mystic, yes. His book of dream interpretation has provided me more insight than anything written for the past thousand years. His is an individuality that attenuates into a corporation of shadows. I became interested in ancient theories of dream interpretation after my sickness . . . after the death of my body and my continued consciousness. Nothing modern spoke to my experience. Not Freud, with his phallus groping. Not some crystal-fetish psychic. One line in particular gives me, for lack of a better word, peace. As if he, too, had lived as I do, or if he had at the very least encountered one like me and attempted to provide some kind of solace. He writes, 'to be dead in dreams announces freedom from anxiety.' When I first read that, it freed me. And once I felt free, I began to write and perform in truth.

"I am dead and this is my dream." He gestured to us as if we were nothing more than phantasms. "Since this line is true, I have complete authority to do as I please."

Mathias turned to Juan.

"But that reminds me of something more mundane. Juan, I know that you can draw. We need a new logo for this band. Desekration is such a stupid name, though I believe in what it means. If I desecrate something, it is because I once believed it to be sacred. Whatever you come up with should convey that."

Svart and Tomi had started packing up their gear. Me too. I mean, you get Juan and Mathias into a conversation, it could go on for hours, each one of them out-monologuing the other. I think Mathias and Juan intrigued each other. They let each other talk, that's for sure.

Goat Song Sacrifice

Mathias approved of Juan's costumes. And Juan admired the way Mathias wore his own body as a costume.

The other thing they had in common was that neither of them liked to be ignored.

Tomi had nearly made it out of the door when Mathias sprung toward him.

"Drummer!" he shouted, and clapped twice to get his attention.

"We are not done here yet. We may have a satisfactory recording of some songs, but we are still missing the most important song. We are missing the goat song, though it must be something that we introduce at this show."

"The goat song?" I asked, even though I knew he'd probably make me feel like an idiot.

I asked even though I felt like I'd been there before. The goat song. The katabasis. And me, the audience for another half-baked mysticism.

Juan cut in and said, "That's what the word 'tragedy' means. In Greek."

"That is true. It refers to sacrifice."

I looked over at Svart and rolled my eyes. He made no reply. He shuffled to the side, away from me. He'd been shamed into subservience. Plus, of course, even he was aware that Mathias had better ideas than anything formulated up in that gigantic cranium of his. Even I knew that, though I tired of my role as the loyal pawn. I was starting to wonder what I could contribute on my own. What idea or riff or phrase would come from me?

"We will write a goat song for the show," Svart said.

"Not *a* goat song. *The* goat song," Mathias corrected. "The song that, in its truth, desecrates the emotions of the listener. The song that reveals the meaninglessness of mortal existence—it makes one aware that the end is only decay."

I'd had enough. I'd been led astray by theories before.

"Sounds great, but what does that mean for us? What's it have to do with metal—with our album?"

"I'll try to make it simpler so that you can understand. I write the words and sing them. The rest of you write the music and play it. My words express this idea. Your songs are not doing that. I want them to. I want them to express this idea on at least one song."

"It makes sense to me," Juan said.

"I want you to make a song that rouses the flesh, that raises the hairs on your arms and neck. I want a song that provokes a physical response. I want a song that makes the body aware of its unavoidable demise. For that is the tragedy of the living."

If I don't have much to tell you about Maria and me—what we talked about, our deepening bond, and that sort of thing—it's because there's not much to say. We didn't share heartfelt opinions on the poetic intricacies of Ostrogoth's back catalogue. We quickly fell into a routine with little variation.

At least once a week, we'd meet up at a bar, drink too much, then wind up in someone's bed. Mine or hers. We fell into a rut. Two animals drinking and rutting and drinking and rutting. We made our own goat song. The horny and the horned. Doggie style was part of the routine, too. Her face to the wall. Her ass in the air. One time, a vicious charley horse gripped my leg—first my thigh, then my calf—just as I kneeled into position behind her. Another time, I came out of the bathroom to find her, naked, lying on her back, her arms and legs raised up like a dead bug's. Each time, no matter what, I did it just the same.

Goat Song Sacrifice

Things weren't going so well for Juan. What I had with Maria counted as a model relationship compared to him and Delphine. I didn't know that, though, until I went over to his place one day for some Belgian burritos.

They're a regional specialty. A recipe we refined that year out of desperation. I mean, prior to our time in Belgium, both of us had subsisted for long periods of our adolescence on Taco Bell and fried Cuban food from crusty walk-up cafés.

It could take you an entire day to assemble the ingredients. The grocery store on the Rooseveltplein carried beans, but not salsa. The Lidl—a kind of Eurowalmart, but smaller—on Juan's side of town carried something they called salsa that had the taste and consistency of ketchup mixed with a few spurts of hot sauce. You had to go to some Middle Eastern food emporium out by the shoe bar, the Dulle Griet, to get anything resembling a tortilla.

Whoever went to the Lidl was responsible for picking up some cans of this cheap beer, Grafenwalder, that cost like fifty cents each. It was even cheaper than Jupiler. I had the beans in my backpack. It was Juan's turn to get the beer. The last few times we did this, he came to my place and I supplied the beer. I hadn't been to Delphine's before. As I rang the doorbell, I wondered if I should have brought some of my own beers, but when Juan opened the door, he handed me a can. He'd been generous since moving in with her.

"Belgian burritos," I said, then popped open the beer.

He had his own can, too. We clinked them together and went inside.

Delphine lived in the kind of apartment I wouldn't have been able to imagine before moving to Europe. It was small and relatively basic. Like mine, it had been furnished with practical minimalism as the key goal. It was larger than my place, though. Let's call it a double slaapkamer. Or a slaapkamer and a half, at the very least. But the thing about it—the reason no renting student would have a place like it at home—is that the windows for each slaapkamer opened out onto a medieval castle.

You could see an abbey from my window, too, but it was in the distance. Delphine paid cheap rent for moat-front property. I would never waste a beer this way, but you could drop your can of Grafenwalder out the window and it would plop into a genuine water-filled moat.

Tourists clamored about on the battlements of the castle. You could hear the click of their cameras across the moat. I mean, besides the obvious fact that we don't have thousand year old castles in the middle of our cities, Americans would have made sure that only the truly rich, and not idiots like me and Juan, could ever afford such a view.

"Dude. You have a castle in your backyard," I said.

"I know." Juan said. "I thought I told you about it. Delphine's place is pretty nice . . ."

He stopped, then pulled a frying pan out of the kitchen cabinet. He handed me the pan. New Juan, the kept man, might hook me up with some beers, but he still expected me to cook.

"It's pretty nice when she's not here," he continued.

"Ah shit." I took a sip. "What's the matter?"

He filled me in. He'd had drama of some sort or other since he moved in.

"It'll be like she's breaking up with me, but then she's not breaking up with me. She'll say I'm too close. That she needs space. But then she'll say I need to woo her."

"Woo her?"

"Right. Like take her to dinner, and buy her flowers, and spend my day strewing fucking rose petals around the place. I'm either supposed to be absent, or else spending all of my time orchestrating an ongoing cycle of romantic gestures. I can't do that. No one can."

I cut to the chase.

"How's the sex?"

"It's . . ." he paused, weighing whether or not to trust me with the next bit. Then, he blurted it out. "She tried to stick her finger up my ass. While we were doing it."

"Yowza!" I squealed, then opened another Grafenwalder. I made a mental note to buy Maria some flowers. To thank her for leaving my anus unprobed. Maria was sounding better and better by the minute.

"Did you let her?" I asked. You never knew with Juan.

"No. Of course not. The worst thing, though, is she's been getting these phone calls late at night. It happened last night. It was like around ten or something. After that, she went out. Said she had to see a friend. She didn't come back until four in the morning. And even then, she slept on the couch."

"Oh." This didn't sound good. "Did you talk to her about it in the morning?"

"No. I pretended to sleep until she left for school."

"Fuck, man. That sucks. These Euros are all a little crazy. Delphine. That dude Mathias," I tried to lighten the mood. "Especially Mathias. He creeps me out."

What Juan said surprised me.

"I actually like Mathias. He's a good guy. Sure, he has his hang ups, but you don't know everything he's been through. He's told me some things. He's given me some tips about Delphine, too."

I didn't know what to say. What bothered me more? That he defended Mathias or that he'd gone to him first with his lady trouble.

"You shouldn't be such a jerk to him," Juan continued. "And I'm not just saying that because he's the most talented guy in the group."

At that point, we heard the rattling of keys in the door lock.

"Oh—that's her!"

Juan ran to the window that overlooked the front door. He popped it open and stuck his head out.

"Delphine!" he chirped.

I could see how she might feel hemmed in by Juan's love.

I poked my head out and waved.

"David's here," Juan said. "We're making dinner."

Delphine waved back, a manic, impossibly fake smile on her face.

Out on the street, something caught my eye. Someone. Some lone guy out there in the crowd of people checking out the restaurants, shops, and bars that lined the street. It could have been the way the guy stopped when Juan called Delphine's name. Stopped, then kept on moving a bit faster. Without turning back. He had a thick mat of black hair. A leather jacket. He moved with a looseness in his hips, each step a kick to dislodge a jangled boot.

I didn't really put it together until I noticed the Mercyful Fate patch on the guy's shoulder. As he disappeared into the crowd I said, just loud enough for Juan to hear, "That was Nekrokor."

17.
A Cough in Darkness

We all took to our assignment, our quest for the goat song, with varying degrees of effort. At first, I didn't want anything to do with it. Juan's katabasizing was still too fresh. Svart's indoctrination efforts, too. And the thing is, I'd bought into both of their ideas. Abandoned songs, styles, things I liked, to fit in, to belong, even though I claimed to be my own person, an individual, a lone man standing alone with my guitar alone to guide me.

The more I tried not thinking about it, the more I thought about it. The underlying challenge, what Mathias had explained to me in, as he said, "simpler" language, appealed to me. He wanted a sound that moved the body, but he described the goat song as something different from the way my old bosses over at Plutonic Records talked about music moving the body. For them, a devastating grind assault moved the bowels. It made them shit. Or at least that's what they said.

I always hated that. I didn't see the guitar as a proctologist's tool. The reason I couldn't just blow off this goat song idea, too, was that Mathias described something similar to how I felt when I listened to his old band, to one song on *The Intrapsychic Secret* in particular. It's that part at the end of "The Inner Sanctum" after the acoustic interlude. When the sound and, especially, Nordikron's voice, return with a vengeance.

Mayhem's "Freezing Moon" has always done something similar for me. Rotting Christ manage it at least twice on *Thy Mighty Contract*. Emperor's "I Am the Black Wizards"—the version on the mini album, though. The split with Enslaved. By the time they recorded it for *In the Nightside Eclipse*, they'd sanitized the riff or something. Lysoled the nekro away.

These few songs evoke the uncanny, the Unheimliche, through sound. Each band somehow found a riff so dissonant and repulsive that, paradoxically, it attracts you to it. Something the body rejects with a shiver, but also wants and anticipates more with every repeated listen.

Could I replicate the sound of a fork scraped across a window, or somehow scratch my guitar pick across a chalkboard and call that a riff? Like those sounds, it had to be found, not made. The way Mathias explained it, the goat song preexisted music. You couldn't come up with it. You had to excavate it from the most primitive crevices of your animal mind.

The spirit of the goat song descended on me one afternoon while I sat in the Vooruit nursing a coffee and studying for my Dutch exam. You conjugate enough foreign verbs and you're in a space between languages, where words in any language are just so many gibberish sounds stacked together like Legos.

Midway through a pile of notecards, I heard it. I intuited it. I hummed a riff as I mouthed the correct forms of each verb on each notecard. This could be it, I thought. A fully formed riff sent from the chthonic realm.

This could be it, I thought until a walk to the counter for an extra sugar packet broke the spell. A techno remix of Twisted Sister's "We're Not Gonna Take It" played on the Vooruit's soundsystem, the guitar buried beneath a frenzied 808. In my verb absorption, I hadn't noticed it. Not consciously.

As the sugar dissolved through the coffee's milky foam, the song faded out into one of those DJ interludes, all airhorns and Missile Command sound effects. I still had the riff stuck in my head, though.

This could be it, I thought.

This could be it, and no one would have to know where I got it. Besides, it had to be better than anything Juan could come up with. It had to be better than anything I could come up with alone. This might as well be it, I thought.

After that, I went home and pecked out the riff on my guitar. I unearthed it. I excavated a power riff from a time when a man could don pink fringed tights without the aid of classical texts and sacrificial rites to explain himself. I only used half the notes, but warped them with the most epileptic tremolo I could muster.

I disguised the riff just enough that no one would recognize it. If the riff were Dee Snyder in his thigh bone gnawing heyday, my embellishments were like a fake moustache plastered right over his blush, his equally fake beauty mark.

Even as I congratulated myself for coming up with something worth playing in practice, I knew it wouldn't work. He'd dismiss it.

The dude doesn't even want a riff, I thought, or anything that could be transcribed into notes.

He wanted our instruments to make sounds, not notes. Like his voice. He wanted us to produce the last strangled cry of a sacrificial goat. A grave worm, not an ear worm.

Svart looked for the goat song in his own way. The next time I went to practice, ready to unveil my twisted riff, he greeted everyone at the door with a stack of concert tickets. A way to regain favor. To make us owe him.

He nearly panted with excitement.

"King Diamond is playing in Brussels! Next week—hoh, I have loved him since I was a kid! My uncle—my mom's brother—he gave me a Mercyful Fate record for Christmas one year. How cool! Satan for Christmas! I played it loudly all day, on my little toy record player, as I sat under the Christmas tree—in the same room you used to call home, David. I bought tickets already, for all of us. This is like, how do you say, on the job training. Attendance is mandatory!"

Mathias, not surprisingly, disagreed. He refused the ticket.

"That is pop music," he said.

Svart sputtered. That was supposed to be his line. He didn't know how to respond to Mathias and his persistent condescension. Svart offered the ticket again, but the guy wouldn't take it. He spun on his heel, his little Batman cape spinning behind him, and walked away.

"Verse, chorus, verse. A solo here and there. Pop music. You can feel the wrong belief in the music itself. I'm not saying that he is unskilled. As craftsmen, King Diamond and whatever troupe of musicians he's managed to assemble for this tour show considerable skill at assembling clever trinkets. The stageshow, I'm certain, will display an ingenuity in keeping with the songs themselves. Like a musical."

Mathias pulled his lyric sheets out of his black leather messenger bag and added "I will be there. I'm on the guest list. I don't need a ticket. Astrampsychos is opening. I am only going to witness their performance. As should you. We are, after all, opening for them shortly."

Everyone but Juan had a deep familiarity with King Diamond. Juan, remember, was a recent convert to metal's cultish devotion. He took the ticket—it was free, after all—but then asked Svart why he thought King Diamond was so great.

"Hah—you are in for a treat!" Svart said, as he pushed a Mercyful Fate tape into the studio console and pressed play. Mathias grimaced, but endured the hated pop music in silence while studying his lyrics.

I mean, the way that Mathias acted wasn't so unusual. Svart liked King Diamond, but he wouldn't let me listen to Ozzy. I still hold onto my theories about which Metallica albums you can listen to and say with a clear conscience that you like metal. I'm a dick. I admit it. And at the time, no one questioned this elitism. It wasn't like now, where everything is cool. Where you get props for showing any interest in music at all. It's just that Svart thought he could reassert his value to the band by taking us all out to a show.

Juan had heard the name "King Diamond," but knew little about him other than the fact that he was popular in the eighties. That decade, for Juan, was memorable more for Morrissey's transition from pompadoured frontman to pompadoured solo artist than King Diamond's development from talented singer to composer of epic, occult metal operas. But Juan came around easily—for one, he loved the costumes, the way that King Diamond performed while dressed like the Victorian characters in his songs.

Svart showed him a picture of King Diamond and Juan said, "Oh wow! He has a hat like mine."

Maybe "loved" is putting it lightly. Juan's exposure to King Diamond marked a turning point for his own costume. Either that, or it just happened to coincide with the inevitable need, with winter drawing near, to buy warmer clothes. Instead of the cheap counterfeit ski jacket I'd recently picked up for forty bucks at an outdoor booth on the Rooseveltplein (it had four stripes and the word "abiban" embroidered in neon green across the chest), Juan showed up at the next practice in a black wool trench coat lined with dark red satin. It stretched to his ankles, where I noticed he'd switched his fringed moccasins for heavy, buckle-spangled motorcycle boots. The whimsical pirate had taken up residence in the House of Usher.

His situation with Delphine might have had something to do with it, too. He hadn't told me what went down after our Belgian burritos. After our Nekrokor sighting.

Juan had on his top hat, too. And, underneath the trench coat, a black pinstriped suit. He looked like Gomez Addams decked out for a ghoulish formal.

The flowers, though. He'd gotten rid of most of them. Only one remained tucked in the brim. And he'd dipped it, the frail flower from a bouquet Gale had given him only a month or so before I met him—for their second anniversary, in a vat of black ink. Its center remained pinkish gray, but the black edges of each petal gave it a charred appearance, like a pink marshmallow bunny skewered then burned as part of a s'more sacrifice.

King Diamond's elaborate face makeup influenced Juan's makeover as well. He'd already taken to wearing Delphine's mascara, but he took it even further. He smeared a thick black crescent under each eye. In his new costume, Juan easily outpaced Nordikron as the most ghoulish, the ghoulishiest, of the crew. The effect was so striking that Nordikron broke out in applause when Juan arrived that night.

"Now this man shows effort. Shows a willingness to unearth the goat song."

With the new costume came a shift in Juan's interests as well. Over the next few weeks, the Juan I knew, with his Joseph Campbell fixation on the monomyth, on the ouroboros itself as the ur-creature lurking below the surface and nibbling at the edges of all cosmologies, of the breathy ocarina whistle as a symbol of humanity's deepest longing for spiritual communion through sound—all of that faded away, replaced by a new set of concerns. So, no more disquisitions on the bulbous shape of the ocarina as an analogue to the round fecundity of the mother goddess. No more ocarina at all. It disappeared for quite some time. Instead, a distinctly new persona emerged, marked by his new stage name. The bard became, at first, the Unholy Bard and, by the time we sent the rough mix of *Infernö* off to Nekrokor, the Bard of Unholy Desires. The costume reflected this new persona, and his new lyrical and musical obsessions marked his immersion in a new role as a decadent Romantic. He even took to hauling around an old, out of tune violin. His little travel guitar disappeared.

This costume, like any of his costumes, was not just for practice. He adopted the new ensemble for trips to the grocery store, errands with Delphine, and, above all, to the goth pub, De Verloren Hemel, where he became a regular fixture, posted up on the arabesqued divan by the window, wine glass in hand. He still stayed with Delphine—they were still always together. It's just that when I saw them, I no longer thought, "The goth and the weirdo. What a perfect match!" Instead, I thought, "You fat whore, you better not hurt my friend."

This new Juan understood Nordikron's obsession with the goat song entirely. Their riffing between songs helped to turn what was some offhand idea in Nordikron's tweaked brain into a dominant structuring idea. I hated it.

At the time, I thought I hated the goat song itself. Why couldn't we just make a sick riff? I thought. One that rocked. But now I realize what I really hated was that I was the outsider once again. Take your "sick riffs" back to shitty Cutler Ridge, where you are also an outsider. Clearly, the Unholy Bard belonged and I did not.

The new costume gave Juan a higher status in the band. Nordikron actually listened to, and sometimes nodded in agreement with, Juan's ideas about the atmosphere of the new songs, which now sounded like this:

"This city is the goat song, the still silence along the canals at dusk, the soft footfalls of yourself, and no one else, reflected by the close, crazily tilted walls rising up on either side of the most remote and forgotten streets and alleyways. The goat song is about uncovering that actual history. What you are trying to do is like the decadents seeking refuge in the sensual pleasures of the past. Like the Marquis de Sade, who found refuge in the interplay of pleasure and pain."

I resisted these changes, these conversations, and kept to my own way of playing as much as possible. My status in the band sank a bit more with every practice. I figured they'd come around. As I constantly reminded myself, I was the only one in that studio who'd worked with a real record label, not just some delusional grimlord. So who were these fools to tell me I wasn't playing "right" because it wasn't in line with their pseudo-mystical posturing?

Their philosophical skirmishes about the goat song as the true essence of total death transmuted into sound versus the goat song as the sensuous pleasure of the reanimation of the past took place while Svart, Tomi, and I focused on the more basic problem of stringing together notes and beats.

That's when a fake Twisted Sister riff comes in useful. Nordikron and Juan agreed that it wasn't the true goat song. It conveyed neither the true essence of total death nor the sensuous pleasure of the reanimation of the past. But they didn't reject it out of hand. They didn't recognize it, that's for sure. It conveyed the true essence of rock, or I thought it did, but in those days, no one cared about that.

It wasn't the true goat song, but Svart and Tomi thought it worked as a good starting point for our tape. You can't lead out with the goat song. You have to conceal it so the listener unearths it, too.

As we packed up, Juan asked me what time he should come by my place so we could bike to the train station. Svart and Tomi both had to work that day, but they said they'd meet us at the station around six. We'd all go to the concert together.

Nordikron stood at the other side of our rehearsal room, shuffling together the sheets scribbled with his lyrics. When he heard Juan say "King Diamond concert," he bristled and called out: "You mean, the Astrampsychos performance. No one cares about that old queen, the headliner."

We asked him if he wanted to meet up at the station, too—I didn't even know if Nordikron owned a bike, and couldn't imagine him, with his slight physique, a mop-headed Mr. Burns, exerting the energy to push a pedal, so I didn't ask if he wanted to ride with us. Besides, I tried to spend as little time with him as possible and, after he sniffed my fever stench the last time he was there, I didn't really want him to cross the threshold into my home ever again. I didn't want him to cross my threshold, or do anything else to it, either. He remained the chief suspect in the mystery of the blood-smeared doorframe.

Mathias said he'd just see us at the show—that he planned to go to Brussels a day or so in advance.

"I have some business to attend to," he added.

This answer satisfied me—I didn't really want him coming along any more than a teenage boy would want an adult chaperone on a date, but I thought inviting him was the polite thing to do. Juan, however, couldn't leave well enough alone, and asked what he had to do in Brussels.

"I may no longer be an active member of Astrampsychos, but I am still in close contact with the others. Besides, I'm curious to see how Goathorn—my replacement—is getting on."

Juan's transformation may have been influenced by King Diamond, but it owed at least as much to Astrampsychos. We thought our heavy metal field trip would be, like any night out with Svart and Tomi, a hard drinking and unthinking good time. But the good cheer we'd felt while swilling half-liter cans of Jupiler on the express train to Brussels faded away as the Astrampsychos show began.

Two huge inverted crosses, each one about six feet tall, flanked the stage. A third one stood behind the drum kit. The stage lights dimmed, but nothing happened for ten minutes or so. Then, someone came out in a black hooded robe, the cowl pulled so low over the face that you couldn't make out anything but the tip of a nose.

Whoever it was carried an enormous torch to the middle cross, lit it on fire, then did the same to the other two. After the darkness of the last ten minutes or so, the sudden flare of fire hurt my eyes. Juan's, too. He covered his face with his forearm.

Goat Song Sacrifice

The robed figure walked off stage. The pounding of a drum—bom-bom-ba-ba-bom—boomed over the speakers in a repetitive loop. The stage was empty except for the burning crosses. Their initial lighter fluid flash abated, but they simmered red hot like branding irons for wayward elephants. If you stared at the stage, then closed your eyes, you could see the imprint of three inverted crosses blazed into your retinas.

The residual heat pushed everyone in the front row back a step or two. I took a big sip of my beer, partly to shield my eyes as I raised the cup to my face, to use the plastic cup as a temporary eye shield as I gulped. The drum drone continued unabated; a single sharp crack, a slammed door or a snapped stick, signaled the next part of the rite. I could see why Nordikron insisted on calling it a 'performance,' rather than a concert. I doubted that faithfully playing the tunes of their latest was necessarily the point for these guys.

Four hooded figures came on stage, each holding the side of a long black box. Pallbearers. A coffin. They set it down in between the burning crosses, then left the stage. The drumming continued. Something about the box captured my eye. As I watched, it seemed to jostle in time with the drumming. At first, I thought I had to be imagining it. I leaned over to Juan and asked him if he saw it, too.

"Yeah, I think someone's in there."

"Look . . . there's a cord running out of it."

And before either of us could track the jumble of cord winding from the coffin to the amp, before we knew for sure that someone with a mic lay beneath its heavy lid, we felt it. An amplified sound like chewing or, as we listened, scratching, filled the silence between each drum beat.

Then, an inhuman shriek pierced the PA. The coffin rocked like some demonspawn cradle. I've listened to lots of shrieking disguised as singing, or singing disguised as shrieking, rather—there's always a line between the two, a clear artificiality marking the shriek as art. As a simulation of a death rattle, and not the thing itself. This passed that line. And as the moments passed, the drumming unabated, the sounds morphed from the wordless shriek that passes for singing in the heavy metal world to a single, clearly discernible word, "Help!" rendered in that anguished tone. No one in the crowd moved, but I'm sure everyone wondered the same thing: how much air is there, exactly, in a tightly shut coffin? Not even one cubic meter, no doubt.

No one in the band came out, either. Instead, the rocking, the screaming, that same prerecorded drum beat—bom-bom-ba-ba-bom—continued.

No one in the crowd moved. Because we thought this was part of the performance. I looked around at the faces of the crowd, all clearly illuminated by the still burning crosses. Nordikron, standing in the middle, but toward the back, grinned widely, serenely, more like he was watching some Colin Firth-fronted romantic comedy than the creepy asphyxiation of his replacement. Then, the shrieks for help turned into a series of ragged, wheezing breaths, of dying coughs, that barely kept time with the beat.

One of the robed pallbearers strolled on stage. Casually, like he was stepping outside to pick up the newspaper on a cool autumn morning. Nekrokor. His head no longer covered. At least he wasn't smiling. I couldn't read his expression. He looked more confused than concerned, his head cocked like someone had asked him a riddle. He got to the coffin, fished around in his robes, and raised a tarnished silver key. Whether this was part of the performance, or he seriously wanted to show someone—the sound guy, Nordikron—that he had it, I couldn't tell. I just wanted him to let the guy out.

Goat Song Sacrifice

Nekrokor fiddled with the lock, raised the lid, then lifted the mic out of the coffin.

He said, "Someone call the ambulance."

The drum beat stopped. The lights came on. Goathorn still lay in the coffin, though one arm hung limply out of the side. The stage lights gleamed on his clammy blue hand. Within minutes, a crew of first responders sprinted on stage, looking wildly out of place with their clean crew cuts and fluorescent yellow fire jackets. One of them sprayed the smoldering inverted crosses with a small, hand-held fire extinguisher. The crew pulled the singer out of the coffin and strapped him to a gurney. One of them held a stethoscope to the guy's chest, nodded at his teammates, and then they streamed out as quickly as they came in, carrying the gurney like some kind of open-topped coffin.

Within half an hour, King Diamond's roadies had swept away all evidence of the ill-fated Astrampsychos performance. Except for the coffin. It sat, open, at the far right edge of the stage for the rest of the night. Instead of a satanic pyromaniac funeral, the coffin shared the stage with a cluttered mass of props and set pieces from King Diamond's biggest albums. A high backed wooden wheelchair in one corner evoked Grandma's haunted chamber in *Them*. The drum kit sat on a platform flanked by a set of four stairs. A baby doll in a high-necked lace dress sat in a tiny crib at the top of the stairs and in front of the bass drum. This, obviously, was the *Abigail* set piece. To the right side of the stage, just a few feet from where I'd staked out a position, a small bench topped with a crystal ball, a Ouija board, and a pack of tarot cards called to mind some of the more enduring numbers from King's earlier days in Mercyful Fate.

I should have been ecstatic, but after Goathorn's near death, King Diamond seemed as innocuous as the Wiggles. He played amidst a giant Baphomet backdrop, a movie-screen-sized banner showing a goat head inscribed in a pentagram enclosed by a circle. During "Come to the Sabbath," King pranced across stage with a black candle in one hand, a white candle in the other. He sang "Welcome Home" while sitting in the decrepit wooden wheelchair. On "Abigail," he even mimicked stabbing the baby doll, the evil Abigail, while laughing maniacally. Then, he tossed the doll over his shoulder so it sailed over the drummer's head and disappeared off stage.

He gave a great concert. But when he left the stage after an encore rendition of "A Dangerous Meeting," it was clearly evident that the best concert couldn't hold a candle—not even a black one—to an Astrampsychos performance.

On the train back to Gent, Svart filled us in on what went wrong. He got all the details from Nekrokor. He'd actually slipped backstage to talk to the guy, and to hand him our rough mix. The singer, Goathorn, was supposed to have a key on the inside, Svart told us. Nestled in the satiny coffin cushion right by his left hand, so he could unlock it, then spring out before he suffered too much.

No one denied that some smothering was supposed to be part of his entrance. The other guys had convinced Goathorn that he needed to do that to prove his equal to Nordikron who, allegedly, they'd actually buried and left in the ground for several hours before a show last summer. When that happened, the rest of the band went out for beers, then came back to excavate Nordikron, who'd suffered no obvious ill effects from his interment.

And the coffin needed to be locked. The plan was to lock Goathorn in the coffin again at the end of the show, then throw the key into the crowd. He'd have his own key, so he could get out once off stage, but the audience didn't need to know that. Whoever got that extra key—and all his friends, too—would definitely become Astrampsychos devotees and, more importantly, customers.

They'd be sure to buy the backlog of demos pressed to 7", hunt obsessively for those ultralimited copies of *Live in Brno* with the printing error, you know, where the black cover came out hot pink, and devote themselves to veneration of *The Intrapsychic Secret.* They'd be sure to do everything necessary so that Despondent Abyss could turn a profit. The whole crowd would.

18.
Metametal:
The λόγος of Logos

You, too can own your very own heavy metal logo. Transform your name into an exposition of evil, a harbinger of power chords, a visual representation of blast beats chattering away at the table of the artist or designer.

Or set to work for some struggling local band. If you produce something evil enough, something with the allegorical heft to cast the souls of band and listeners both to the fated shores of Lemuria, something evocative of a pandaemonic maelstrom, something reminiscent of a Ouija scrawled message from beyond the gate of death, something approximating the Nekronomikon's occult blueprints, then you can garner a bit of immortality yourself, secure yourself a spot in the record sleeve or CD booklet, a tiny mark of eternity and veneration, somewhere between the sound engineer and the executive producer.

For making a simple logo.

But it's more than a logo, isn't it? More than a crass marketing doodle. Instead, it's an icon, an ikon, an attempt to render the transcendent in pictographic form. The ideal logo transfers the band in question from this earthly sphere and into the constellations of the cosmos. Where do you think that bus hurled Cliff Burton anyway? Toward Orion.

It stellifies them, like the heroes of ancient myth, snatches them from this humble sphere and splatters them across the outermost surface of Ptolemy's crystal spheres like a horde of locusts across the windshield.

It started with Zeppelin, with the symbols attached to each player, with symbols evoking essence. One is the cloth, another the hand that sews tight. The symbols do more than name each musician; they name the glimmer of eternal essence, that divine spark the Greeks called λόγος, or logos, or Word, that animates a finite performance, that limited period of time while the music plays, and joins it with the spirit's harmony of infinite tones.

The symbol, the logo, obliterates the name.

Robert Plant's icon, the feather in the circle, can be interpreted as an elaboration of this statement. The feather signifies that which is bygone, that which has been propelled by the breath of the spirit as it moved over the waters. The feather is the tongue of air as flame is the tongue of fire. And yet the immaterial feather, as light as flame, as heavy as dew, is not the only thing moved by the logos. The hall will fall as the hill will fall. The hill will spill headlong into the sea. The feather is the wind and that which is moved by the wind. It is the sign of a forgotten land, its people pushed by wind into the pull of the sea. The feather in the circle symbolizes not just a mussmopped Celt sauntering across stage in a gilded kimono. It symbolizes, Robert Plant has said, the ancient deity that impelled the people of Easter Island, the Mu civilization, to destroy themselves through the creation of chiseled timeless monoliths.

The logo contains the λόγος. The Word consumes the word.

19.
Logocentrism

Juan's assignment—making a new logo—tormented him. Or, rather, Svart tormented him as he tried to draw something that somehow surpassed the perfection Svart believed he had achieved with his, as he had only recently admitted, "Destruction-influenced" design:

I ran into Juan one day as I walked home from a final exam review for Dutch class. He'd spent the whole afternoon holed up in the Vooruit with a pad of paper, a host of art supplies, a stack of *Kerrang!* back issues, and the bellicose art coaching of a caffeinated Svartikles downing endless cups of Douwe Egberts.

"I'd never realized how ... how ... logocentric that magazine is!" he said. I'd missed Svart by just a few minutes. He'd abandoned Juan in a rage of frustration. Whatever Juan drew, it wasn't right. For hours, Svart guided him through the stack of magazines, page after page, his corn cob finger pounding band logos in ads, record reviews, interviews.

"Every page had some detail—a letter shape, a font color, an arcane symbol—that he wanted me to emulate, but not imitate. I must have burned through about five different markers. Worst of all, he kept changing his mind. One minute, he definitely wanted the logo to ride over a goaty Baphomet, so I'd draw it. Then he'd totally freak out, asking me if I thought Desekration was just going to be some pale imitation of some obscure band from Greece where he'd got the idea to begin with. Look at this . . ."

Juan spread out the ruffles in his white smock. Brown flecks spotted the shirt.

"The guy started spitting coffee at me. Just spraying it through his big, buffoonish lips."

"Why'd he do that?"

"Let me ask you something—how do you spell 'Desekration'? The band—our band—not the actual word."

I told him. Just like it's spelled here. He then recounted Svart's vehement insistence it was actually supposed to be "Desekratttion," the trinity of "t"s inverted, of course, to reflect the "unholy union" unleashed by the mind meld of its two most important and, by his reckoning, famous members: Nordikron and himself.

I knew it had been rough. I'd stopped by earlier that day on a lunch break. Dutch lunch. On the walk down, I'd spotted Tomi, carrying a duffel bag and decked out in a form fitting purple and yellow spandex suit. It looked like a weightlifter's outfit, or the sartorial offspring of a leotard and a pair of biker shorts. If he had a headband, he could have been Olivia

Newton John's stunt double. I asked him where he was going.

He pointed down a nearby drive that ended in an arched entrance to a three-story building. Two red and white banners hung down each side of the arch, emblazoned with a word we hadn't learned, but sounded like a good band name: "Powerzaal."

"Spinning class."

Tomi jostled his duffel bag and headed up the drive.

"To work out."

Once I got to the Vooruit, I saw Svart in action. In the time it took me to eat a kleine boterham and down a Fanta, he did just about everything but cop a squat on the zinc-topped café table and unfurl a steaming load on Juan's vast pile of sketches:

"No. That's gay."

A sugar packet hurled in Juan's face.

"Why are you drawing a fucking garden gnome? No."

A loud, irritated sigh.

"This is shit."

The rusty squeal of chair legs against the terrazzo floor.

"Excuseer. So shit I must make a shit."

Svart's finger pounded an ad.

"This looks like the Master's Hammer logo, but not as interesting. Where is the originality?"

That's around the time I headed back to class.

A few days later, I saw Nekrokor again. In the nachtwinkel. He was with Nordikron.

Mathias and Bård, Bart and Matt. Two old pals. They stood side by side in front of the beer case.

It was the same nachtwinkel I always went to. The one by the Record Huis.

I'd slipped in to pick up a blikje as a post-exam reward. It was only afternoon, not quite three, but I deserved it. I had just passed Nederlands niveau een.

I knew that because Helena nearly complimented me in the last part of the exam, an oral interview with her. After I answered her final question. I had described, in grammatically impeccable Dutch, my childhood relationship with Simon, the family cat my sister named at the height of her Duran Duran phase. When I finished, Helena looked up and said, "Uitstekend. I didn't think you—I didn't think an American—could do it. I hope you sign up for level two in January."

I didn't commit to more Dutch. I smiled and gathered my stuff. My backpack and jacket. I left before she could rethink her evaluation. It's not like it mattered if I passed or not. My mastery of Dutch would not shape my destiny.

But I liked using the language when I wandered the city. When I stopped into a nachtwinkel to buy beer, for example. I liked interacting with people who had no opinions on the merits and flaws of the Celtic Frost back catalogue.

My post exam elation faded when I saw them. No way to escape undetected, my blikje safely tucked away in my backpack. I should have gone up to them. To him. Nekrokor. I mean, what had he done to me besides give me a chance?

And a crucified bug. And a disgusting wart finger. A weird postcard, too. Still—I should have shown him I wasn't fazed. I should have greeted him with a "What's up?" and a firm handgrip. Like my dad taught me.

Of course he was going to haze me a bit. Make me feel uncomfortable. That's, like, the root of male friendship. It's not as though my old friends, my Valhalla bandmates, gave me footrubs and brought me bonbons. They could be dicks, too. One time John gave me an Ex-Lax brownie. Just to fuck with me. And even Svart's neverending pub crawls were just another form of initiation based around a simple premise: let's see how wasted the American guy can get.

But I didn't go up to them. I just wanted a drink. It could have been the way they glared at the beer case—Nekrokor, arms crossed over his leather jacket, over his spikes and patches, frowned at the beers as though they'd done him some unnamed wrong. As though the store's beer selection was unbefitting a true nekrowarrior of Armageddon. Mathias looked down at his feet. He had on his Velcroed cape and a sleeveless shirt, his arms as pale white as a frog's belly.

It didn't seem like they'd care about my test. My achievement in the face of monolinguism. They'd probably say I should be practicing guitar. Or lying in a ditch, practicing death. Getting ready—in some way—for the Desekration show a few nights away. And they'd be right. I planned to practice. Once I had my beer.

In other words, they didn't look like the fun brigade. Even though Mathias probably needed a beer more than Nekrokor did. More than I did. He seemed so frail, so cold, like he'd just disintegrate into a little pile of brittle snow.

Once I fully realized that they stood between me and the beer, I thought, "Fuck it. I'll just go to the grocery store instead." It was only a block or so down the street. It had better beers, too. Piraat, Grimbergen, Orval. But then they pulled some bottles out of the case and moved to the cash register. They moved toward the door.

I quickly slipped into the rows of snacks. With my abiban jacket and backpack, I looked like everyone else. A student. A person bundled up against a cold day. Abiban's a popular brand in Belgium. And I displayed no outward signs of metal identity. A plain black stocking cap covered my hair, its fringes tucked into the jacket's collar.

I studied the store's selection of potato chips—perverse

Euroflavors like ketchup, pickle, and horseradish—figuring they'd be gone in a few minutes.

The guy at the register had that typical Belgian demeanor. One I'd never be able to pull off, not even if I lived here for a decade and brainwashed myself daily with Jacques Brel songs. He had short dark hair with a Clark Kent side part. Olive skin. A distant nonexpression. He regarded Mathias and Bård with an aloof and good humored detachment. He recognized their ridiculousness—Bård in his spikes and leather, Mathias in his nekrosuperhero getup—but chose not to show it.

He rang up their order. Eight bottles. And one box of chamomile tea.

Mathias coughed, then pointed at the price on the register. I guess it didn't match what was listed on the cooler.

He asked the guy about it in Dutch, but the guy said he couldn't understand him.

He asked again, and the guy switched to English. I encountered this move a lot. It was the prime reason to consider level two. But Mathias, I thought, was an insider. A multilingual Euronative adept at navigating beer case inventory across the continent. Nachtwinkel or nightshop, it makes no difference. They share a historic grammar. I mean, Svart always went on and on about how great Mathias spoke Dutch.

The clerk said something to another guy working the winkel, who snickered then went back to unloading a box of popcorn-flavored potato chips. It was something about Limburgers. I couldn't quite make it out. Maybe we'd get to regional insults in level two?

I had to look it up later. He called Mathias a midget Limburger. *Dwerg*. A dwarf. He charged him the higher price, too. Mathias didn't argue. Instead, Nekrokor fished some coins out of his jacket to make up the balance.

After he took the money, the clerk put their stuff into a plastic bag. Before they left, Mathias took the box of tea out of the bag and secreted it away in his cape.

20.
The True Sigil of Desekration

Juan came over a few nights after that. For Belgian burritos. He'd called earlier in the day to see if he could come over. He said Delphine wouldn't be back until late. She was out with some friends. He said he'd bring drinks, too. Besides, he wanted to show me his designs. For the Desekration logo. He had it nearly figured out. And Nordikron wanted him to make some flyers for the show.

I was excited to see Juan. I wanted to tell him about my most recent Nekrokor sighting. Until I let him in. He didn't bring any beer. He only had a wine bottle or something in his hands. Even worse, he brought Mathias along.

I wanted to shake Juan. Tell him burrito night was not to be fucked with. I felt really angry.

His costume kind of added to it all. I mean, I told you about it. The long trench coat. The clunky boots. The black make up smeared beneath his eyes, each day the shadows growing a bit longer.

Sometimes, like on burrito night, I didn't want to hang with a costume. And I definitely didn't want to hang with Mathias, who shuffled behind in the hallway. He had on his usual

160

cape and t-shirt combo. An old Venom shirt. No jacket or anything, even though it had been freezing every day for the past week.

Mathias surveyed the scrubbing I'd given the doorframe. He didn't say anything about it, but he was pretty conspicuous. After I invited them in, he wiped his finger against the doorframe. Then he sniffed his finger, his mouth open as he sniffed. Like a cat.

That was another thing—a part of the new costume. I had to formally invite them in. You know, like, because they're vampires of imperial blood.

After I opened the door, I said, "Hey, what's up dudes?" then went back to cutting a tomato. The front door opened directly into the kitchen.

Juan was real obvious about it: "Aren't you going to invite us in?"

"I did. Come on in."

I guess that was formal enough, because then they walked past me. Juan set the bottle on the kitchen table. When they passed through the kitchen, I nearly choked on their rank body odor. Showers, you know, are a modern convenience and so unnecessary to the eternal undead.

I made a concerted effort not to cut my finger with the paring knife. No need to incite some sanguinary frenzy. And I found myself thinking Juan was faking it. Thinking that the lugubrious archduke of melancholy arriving, sans beer ... that wasn't the real Juan. And then catching myself. So who *is* the real Juan? The Caribbean scallywag I'd met—not that long ago—in Booksalot? I wondered how well I really knew Juan. Or what claim I had on him, other than we came from the same place. Uncle Luke came from that place, too, but that didn't make us spiritual brothers.

"What's that?" I asked, gesturing to the squat black bottle

Juan had put on the table.

"Port," he said. It had a wax seal around the cork.

It looked fake. Like a movie prop. Like him. The bottle the castaway pirate boy uses to launch his secret message, his last plea for help. The bottle the besotted marquis drains in the drawing room before he deflowers the chambermaid.

"Port?" I asked, after reading the label. And the price tag.

It wasn't cheap. Worth at least a dozen blikjes.

The bottle had a picture of, like, Zorro or something. Of a scene from a Juan and Mathias costume party—one top hat plus one cape equals an incredibly suave gentleman. Or at least that was my impression. I mean, now I know— Sandeman. That's some luxe drank. At the time, though, I was just happy I had some beers of my own. So I didn't have to drink Napoleonic Robitussin.

"You have some glasses?" Juan asked.

I got down two. I figured I'd at least try it.

"I need one, too," Mathias said.

I shrugged and grabbed a third one. I'd never seen him drink before.

He ate a burrito, too. It didn't have meat, so it didn't conflict with his weird vampiric vegetarianism. He didn't even pull out his little blood bottle. And he nearly ate the whole thing.

Juan said he had a few things to finish before he showed us his designs. He set up his sketchbook, pens, and charcoal on the kitchen table while I washed the dishes. Mathias went out on the terrace.

After I put the dishes away, I went out to find him. Juan said he was nearly done.

"You good out here?" I asked as I stepped outside. It wasn't windy or anything, but the cold immediately seeped into your bones.

"There a full moon or something?" I quipped.

As much as he creeped me out—maybe because he creeped me out—I couldn't restrain myself from making sarcastic comments. Call it a defense mechanism. After seeing him in the nachtwinkel, though, I realized I wasn't the only one with those impulses. Something about him brought it on. It's like he expected it, even though deep within he regarded us all—nachtwinkel clerks and disposable guitarists all—as so many human mice, everyone but maybe Nekrokor clearly inferior to his self-constructed grandeur.

"Don't be obtuse. I don't peddle in Scooby Doo clichés. Not like your favorite pop star. Not like King Diamond. Tonight is a new moon. A dead moon. Shrouded in the shadow of this floating tomb."

I shivered. The tip of my nose burned from the cold. I leaned against the railing. Not too far, though. I'd advise against putting yourself in any kind of compromising position with Nordikron lurking near.

In the sky, you could just make out the flat black disc of the new moon hanging above the abbey's steeple.

He asked how old I was, then said, "Maybe it is because I am . . . because this body . . . is a few years older than you that I see through his thin façade. His so-called Satanism."

"I thought you'd like that," I said. The sarcasm. I couldn't help it.

He laughed, flashing a row of crooked tombstone teeth.

"It is the wrong idea of Satan. His is the Satan of this world, a simple inversion of customary morality. Do you know he is ordained in Anton LaVey's Church of Satan?"

"Really?" I wasn't sure what that meant. That between tours, witches hired the guy to preside over white weddings? To eulogize at the funerals of dearly departed warlocks? I wasn't sure what that meant, or why it mattered.

"Yes . . . it is so ridiculous."

"Why?" Again, I thought he'd like that. It's not like King Diamond led a double life as a Baptist deacon or something.

"The followers of Anton LaVey, with their 'Do What Thou Wilt' naked cocktail parties—heavy on the cock from what I've heard—they do not see the truth. Do what thou wilt is not a liberation, an excuse for amoral license. It is a true proposition—yes, do what thou wilt, but only because of the utter nothingness underlying your meaningless actions, underlying the whore you've paid to defile her body as an altar. It is all nothingness. If they knew that, their social club would surely close."

At moments like this, I most regretted my sarcastic digs at Mathias. Not just because of the wide chasm between his grim self-concept and his inept handle on life outside of metal's fantasyland, but because of the sense that he would one day seek to close that gap, to right all the perceived wrongs against him. When you talked to him, you could tell that any action he disapproved of was, to him, done against him. King Diamond wasn't just a fool who tried to live the escapism of his lyrics, he was a fool who dissed Mathias by doing so.

Even if it just meant being taken slightly more seriously in the band, or atoning for whatever vast record of my many wrongs he'd tabulated in his twisted little head, I wanted to keep Mathias talking. I wanted him to see me as someone he could confide in. Someone he could sip port with while admiring the cosmic nonevent of a moonless night.

It seemed to be working for Juan.

"So you don't believe in, like, I don't know," I gestured toward the sky, "the beyond?"

"Oh, there is a beyond," he answered immediately, pulling himself up by the metal railing. "There is a great, all-consuming nothingness. What we call ghosts, the supernatural, exist as incursions of that chaos. It feels colder than ice. Colder," he turned to me, "than even this autumn night feels to you.

He took a sip of his port, then grimaced before swallowing.

"The coldness cares nothing for ceremonies, ridiculous pseudo-rituals. It is neither for nor against individual action. It is the coldness of the shadow that joins the earth to the moon. The coldness of the dreaming dead. Of those alive who sleep in death."

Mathias drained the rest of the cup. He emitted a high-pitched wheeze when he swallowed. A congested Nazgul cough. Just like the one he does at the beginning of "Selva Oscura." Then he stepped back into the apartment. He wobbled just the slightest bit. The lightweight.

"Oh, this is too much for a social call. An impromptu dinner party. I hope you don't mind that Juan invited me along. We've become fast friends."

"Oh—uh. No worries, man."

Inside, Juan sat bent over the kitchen table, frantically scribbling. Random scraps of paper hung out of the sketchpad. Various pens and sticks of charcoal rolled around the table, shifting as he drew. He adjusted the port bottle every so often, turning it a micrometer to the left, a micrometer to the right. He still had a full glass, though; he seemed to be drawing the bottle or something. The Zorro guy.

Mathias went over to my little practice area. He sat in the brown pillowchair and pulled out my keyboard. He turned it on and tested out its various sounds. He eventually settled on the most generic synthesizer tone. "Jump" or "Separate Ways." Then he started playing an endless two-note progression. Just A flat, then D with his right hand. He held a chord of the two notes with his left hand, occasionally replaying it.

I figured Juan would take his bottle with him when he left, so I committed to drinking more than my fair share. I refilled my port, drank it, then refilled again. Mathias keyboarded the whole time. He sat with his eyes closed, the synthesizer on his lap. He kind of sang-sighed the notes to himself.

"Meditating?" I asked. Again with the sarcasm.

He peeped his eyes open and answered my question with a question.

"Is this still for sale? You said it was the last time I was here."

"Well, not the last time, was it?" I asked, cocking my head. The doorframe hadn't bled on itself.

He didn't say anything about the door. The blood. He just asked again if he could buy the keyboard.

"Yeah, man," I said. "I don't use it. Svart won't let me."

"That may change," Mathias replied. He pulled a wallet out of his cape and haggled me down to about fifty bucks. I put the money in my pocket.

Juan called us over to the kitchen. He held his hand over his sketchbook, then unveiled a pretty generic logo. He'd drawn the band name in Old English font, but kind of mashed the letters together.

It looked better than Svart's version, where he took some Scotch tape and a pair of safety scissors to the Destruction logo. Juan added a burning pentagram wedged at the top of the "k" and an inverted crucifix for extra evilness. He embellished some of the letters so they looked like Nekrokor's jacket. I wasn't shocked. Just surprised. It didn't seem like the kind of thing Juan—my Juan—would make. And I wasn't sure why it had taken him so much time and effort. He'd spent an anguished week or so on it. It's not too hard to plop a pentagram on something. I mean, no one had computers then. He didn't. But still. My lack of awe must have been obvious. He explained what he'd done:

"I wanted it to look more like an image than a word. That's what I kept thinking about. The spikes and curves make the letters look like the Gulden Draak."

"Hunh," I said. That seemed like a stretch to me. I reached for the port bottle. Mathias, on the other hand, made a serious face, then kind of grabbed the air with both fists. Mathias approved.

"I did something else. For the flyer."

He flipped through some drawings stacked next to the bottle.

The sheet he pulled out was stiff as parchment, its surface thick with dried ink, charcoal, and chalk.

Below the logo, it showed a figure like the Sandeman Zorro, but with a beak. It looked like an old woodcut, but he must have drained a few pens filling it in even more. Underneath a wide brimmed hat, the figure was a black beaked shroud, an inky outline with a surface jagged by a hundred thorns, a hundred tongues of blackest flame.

And that's the moment I choked, my sip of port briefly excoriating the deepest roots of my nostrils.

What he'd drawn—it looked almost exactly like the image from my dream. My fever dream. When I had the curry shits. The fever dream I always had whenever I had a fever.

Whenever I have a fever. It still haunts me today. Gonzo. Nekrogonzo. The somnolent skeksis that, when I'm down and out, regales me with its message of human worthlessness.

I hadn't shared the dream with Juan. And definitely not Mathias. I tried not to think about it ever. I forgot about it until, due to a virus or a poor dietary decision, it visited me anew.

"Wait ... is that?" I asked, but then Mathias cut in. He knew exactly what Juan had drawn.

"The plague doctor," he said.

"I thought it matched the album's concept," Juan explained.

"Our concept?" I asked. This was news to me.

"Of the black plague," Mathias hissed. "An excellent choice."

"I've been telling Mathias about the ouroboros," Juan said. "My painting of it. How we played toward it, let it guide our songwriting."

"A sigil," Mathias said.

"Hunh," I said again through my glass. I realized I was the only one still drinking. These two, I thought, looking at the inky puddles blotted across Juan's sketch pad, nothing good can come from these two together.

"It's an image," Juan explained, "used in alchemy."

"Magic," Mathias interjected.

"It's an image of transformation," Juan said.

I tapped my temple with my index finger and said, "I remember."

The old Juan hadn't disappeared. Not entirely. He never did, despite whatever costume he wore. The triple goddess still roamed in his heart. My awareness of that fact cheered me up a bit. I wasn't really alone, I thought. The only guy without facepaint, antique clothing, or a cape.

As Juan and Mathias hovered over my crumb covered kitchen table and discussed the occult powers of a gig flyer, though, I realized a few things. First, while my Valhalla earnings had been just enough, as my old bandmate had said, to buy a microwave oven, I'd be lucky if Desekration brought me enough for a fucking Hot Pocket. Second, I was definitely the only person among my new bandmates who cared about such mundane concerns. I shouldn't have been surprised. Juan didn't need money. He only needed someone around him to have money. And he had her. Even if everyone else had her too.

They really got going there for a while, entering a mind meld of plagues, sigils, and the shared conviction that every visual and aural emanation of the band must hereafter proclaim total death. Juan eventually gathered his art supplies. The bottle, too. It was empty, though. I'd taken care of that while they talked.

Mathias wrapped the cord around the keyboard and maneuvered it out into the lobby. Before I shut the door, he turned and said, "You weren't supposed to wash it off. The blood. That invalidates its protective properties."

21.
Window Dressing

Someone shattered the nachtwinkel window. Well, maybe "shattered" is too strong of a word. A fissured spider web, about chest high, whorled out from the "t" in "nachtwinkel" on one of the plate glass windows that fronted the shop. The cracked area had the circumference of a basketball, but one or two tendrils arched out and across the whole thing.

I stopped in to get a Glucozade. The port packed a heavy hangover. I needed electrolytes. Inside, neither of the guys seemed concerned about the window. The cashier had the same unflappable mien, every hair in place, his whole body permapressed. The other guy was with him behind the counter. He was stocking cigarettes. They both had their eyes on a Belgian talk show playing on a TV hanging in the corner. Some exposé on the VAT or something. The kind of thing relegated to a 2 AM slot on C-SPAN at home.

I used my Dutch. The cashier did, too. Maybe my hungover voice, my affectless hungover face, made me more Belgian, I thought. Until he handed back my change. He counted it out. In English. Then said, "Have a nice day."

It was past noon. I'd spent part of the morning lying in

bed and staring at the white ceiling as I regretted my decision to kill Juan's port bottle.

I spent the second half of the morning staring at the white balcony. It had snowed overnight. A thick layer of snow sat on the round patio table, making it look like a Double Stuf Oreo with the top cookie twisted away.

I had only seen snow once before. Visiting Midwestern grandparents as a kid. Still, it didn't surprise me. Not like autumn's sudden defoliation. I'd been expecting this next weather stage. When people in Miami mention snow, they're generally not talking about the weather. But I'm a fast learner.

My plan for the afternoon was to wander around until the Glucozade took effect. Look at the snow. Play weather tourist. I had a vague hankering for McDonald's, too, though I'm ashamed to admit it. I was ashamed to admit it to myself. There was a McDonald's right off the center square. It looked out on the Korenmarkt and stood catty-corner from the artsy jazz bar where Svart and I first met Tomi.

Besides, I followed a primarily liquid diet. Coffee for breakfast, beer for dinner. Repeat as necessary. I'm not the kind of guy who needs a Happy Meal. Or so I told myself as I threaded through the streets to the Korenmarkt, along the way even convincing myself I *needed* to go to the McDonald's. Just to take a piss. The Glucozade runs like an ever flowing stream. Everywhere else, you have to pay to pee, a transaction that any American, no matter their political leanings, regards as treasonous and antithetical to the principle of personal liberty.

As I turned to go down Veldstraat, which spits you out on the Korenmarkt right in front of the golden arches, I even pulled out my wallet to count my cash. I had enough for a Big Mac meal. An ice cream cone, too, if I wanted.

It's shameful, I know. Euroreaders, your stereotypes are true.

But I told myself the money was for the bookstore nearby. I'd go there postpiss. Maybe improve my mind. Read up on the occult. See if Mathias was right, the Satanist's anti-Satanic diatribe.

The snow didn't slow me down. Or anyone else. People still whizzed past on bikes and hauled shopping bags out of stores. To me, though, the snow made the city feel even quieter, even smaller. The gray clouds, the brief flurries as I walked, enveloped the city like felt. It dawned on me that I'd spend the holidays in Gent. That in a month or so, I might just buy Nordikron a Christmas present. It seemed crazy.

The snow, the wafting aroma of fries, the promise of a free drink refill for dine-in customers, it was all too much. As you can probably guess, I walked straight into the McDonald's.

I stomped my feet on a golden arch doormat, then went to the bathroom. My piss golden arched into the urinal. I dribbled a bit on the floor, too. Marked this little piece of Belgium as mine, as a tiny American colony. After that, I went right up to the counter and placed my order for a Big Mac meal. In English. I didn't even bother with a "dank u wel." It felt good.

And the Big Mac tasted even better than they do at home. It didn't seem possible. Isn't each all-beef patty a mechanized assemblage, a little meat coaster smashed together from a hundred different cows, but basically the same as any other? I pondered this as I stared out a big window onto the Korenmarkt and chewed contentedly.

The snow slowly covered the square. And out there, at the Korenmarkt tram stop, Maria stood huddled against the cold. I hadn't talked to her in a few days. But that didn't matter. I didn't need to talk to her all the time. It's not like talking was a key component of our relationship. If you'd call it that. Sometimes I needed a few days to reload after we "talked."

I wondered if I should catch her before the tram showed up. Maybe she'd want to head back to my place? So we could "talk." But I still had half a burger and most of my fries. And I had no intention of losing my free soda refill.

She held a bundle of tissues to her face. She may have been sick. A cold or something. And a good reason to stay away. I didn't need any germs.

She kind of shook, too, like she was coughing.

Or crying, I figured as I dipped a fry into some ketchup.

She held the tissues to her chest, revealing cheeks as red as a baboon's ass.

Definitely crying. Could be her period, I thought, then washed the fry down with a sip of Coke. Or PMS. They always leak tears first. Definitely not my problem.

I picked up my tray and moved to a different table. Away from the window.

So I could eat in peace.

Later that afternoon, I passed the Record Huis on my way home. Svart stood outside taping a poster against one of the store's windows.

"Svartikles!" I yelled, then headed over to him.

He didn't wave or anything. He just turned his head and nodded. Snow spattered the shoulders and back of his jacket. With one hand, he held down the right edge of the poster. He held out his left hand and gestured to someone around the corner—a coworker or something—who then passed him a strip of packing tape.

He secured the poster then stepped away to survey his

work. A line of posters wound across the bottom of the window, and the window curved around the corner. If you were sitting across the street at the Vooruit, you'd have no excuse not to notice them. The poster proclaimed our gig, but you'd have to get pretty close to notice that. Besides the time and place of the show, it listed the logo of some other band from Liège called Morbid Mastication and the new, Juan-designed Desekration logo. Hot off the press. Most of the poster, though, consisted of one word, Astrampsychos, the name of the important band and not the extraneous support.

"We've been busy," Svart said, and pointed down Sint Pietersnieuwstraat, which heads right to the Frontline.

A line of posters stretched down the street along any available wall space. The name Astrampsychos stood out, a foot high and a yard long, each letter sprouting tendrils that pushed like a single root through the Gentian streets:

The "A" merged into the "S" in a constant stream of letters, a Chinese dragon lurching through the city. Down the block and across from the language school, it covered the middle of the drinkyoghurt posters that sustained my erotic fantasies and snaked right across the bare breasts of each yogurt-gulping model.

Not the titties! I thought, horrified.

AstrampsychosastrampsychosastrampsychoS, the scrolling name blotted the landscape like some kind of Rorschach infestation that I immediately interpreted as a sign, a tangible manifestation, of a future failure set to arrive in a few short days.

The other guy said, "We could use your help," and stepped around the corner.

"If you're not too busy, of course," he continued. It was Nekrokor, but I'm sure you knew that. I didn't. He's like Grover. The monster at the end of this book. The one who's been there all along. He held an industrial-sized roll of tape in one hand and his knife in the other. I braced myself.

"Or is that asking too much of you?" he sneered.

"No . . . of course not," I said.

He wasn't fucking around. And he let me know it.

"This guy is scared of me," he said to Svart, who stood by with his arms crossed. "A weakling among true men. And what have I done to him?"

Svart's lower lip stuck out in a bouncer's grimace.

"I gave you a chance," Nekrokor said. "But from what I've heard, you haven't taken it seriously, choosing to spend your time having quite a nice time. I've heard that you're going to school and enjoying your nice little place, where you throw vegetarian dinner parties."

"Hohoh!" Svart laughed like a fat and jolly elf. A nekro-santa equally amused and disturbed by such naughty behavior.

"Yeah—vegetarian," Nekrokor went on. "And when he's not doing that, he's writing fucking postcards."

He pointed at me with the tape hand, not the knife hand. It was still menacing.

"I gave you a chance. This isn't a summer camp, or a band camp, or something. I mean, this isn't just about what you do on your 'free time,' although, to truly be in this band, to be on this label, means that you have no free time and that you are not free; instead, it means that you are free to spread our message not just by how you play, but by how you live."

176

He spouted out some total death philosophizing. At one point, he said, "Svart here, he understands that. He lives a life of total death."

Svart, of course, scowled appropriately. But I had to wonder—since I'd lived Svart's life of "total death"—how someone whose mom washed and folded each graying band shirt and every pair of camo cargo pants qualified as a paragon of Nekrokor's nihilistic virtues.

"When I see the two of you standing next to each other," Nekrokor said, "it doesn't even look like you're in the same band. Svart here is ready for battle. You, though, you look like you're ready for a sporting event or something. A basketball game. What the fuck are you even wearing?"

Svart laughed. I had on my usual clothes, my abiban jacket and my winter hat. It was winter and I felt cold. What was I supposed to wear?

He sheathed his knife, then he dropped the tape into a plastic bag filled with posters.

"I've heard the rough mix as well, and, given the company you keep, you should be thankful that it shows promise. And yet I hear them clearly in every song."

I asked him what he meant.

"The derivative riffs," he said. "I pointed them out to Svart. You heard them too, didn't you?" he asked and Svart nodded.

"They suck," Nekrokor added and held his hands up to his head in true frustration.

The wart crater in his palm oozed a treacly fluid.

"You're not on my label to resurrect antique hair metal."

"Oh." He meant my twisted riff. "That one. I can explain . . ."

He pointed at me and I shut up.

"You remember that insect? I sent it as a kind of motivation because you seem like someone who needs that sort of thing. I now realize it was more of a premonition of what you'd do with the opportunity I gave to you."

"Let's go," Svart said.

Nekrokor tilted his head and stepped up to me.

"Just remember that you are the least," he said. "You are expendable. You are behaving like a pest, like undeserving vermin, but this music is not for the lowly. It is for the elite," he clenched his fist—the wart hand—"and its creation demonstrates our power."

I stepped back, slipping a little on the snow.

"Now take some posters," he said as he shoved the plastic bag into my chest, "and do something useful for once."

22.
Doors at Eight, Show at Nine

The night of the show, I stood in my apartment. Glued in place. I had on my clothes. One of my two pairs of jeans. An Unleashed shirt, the least rank victor of a haphazard sniff test.

My lame jacket, my stupid hat.

The snow had mostly melted, but a thin shell of ice coated the railing on the deck outside.

All I really wanted to do was take a few aspirins and call it a night. I had a legitimate headache. Not a hangover. I blamed it on nerves.

I blamed it on the poster. It hung on the door of my Ikea dresser thing. The last one from the stack I taped around town at Nekrokor's request. I stood glued in place even though I was late. We were set to play in one short hour. It said so at the bottom of the poster. Doors at Eight, Show at Nine. In Belgium, even Christ-raping black metal follows an efficient and timely schedule.

Svart was there already. Juan and Tomi, too. Earlier that afternoon, Svart had called to offer me a ride. He had his mom's car and was headed to help Tomi and Juan move their gear.

I told him I'd just walk. The Frontline wasn't far.

That was hours ago.

I mean, it's not like I had stage fright. I'm not going to lie and say that playing a gig never makes me nervous. Performing makes everyone nervous. It's just that playing guitar is one of the few things where nerves kind of shock me into doing the right thing. Playing the right notes. If I had that with sports, I might have been the basketball galoot I looked like out there on the streets of Gent. According to Nekrokor.

The right notes. According to Nekrokor, all my notes were wrong. And I looked wrong while I played them. I did not convey the true spirit of total death. Not like everyone else. No, that couldn't be right, I thought as I put my guitar in its case. He picked me for his label. And not that long ago.

He'd have a different opinion after we played. I'd hit the right notes. He'd see Juan struggle to keep up with any notes. He'd feel the effect of our songs.

And then he and his band would obliterate them all, I concluded. I sat down in my little recliner and fiddled with my wart. A tiny flap of salicylic acid scorched skin the size and shape of a mondo booger curled off my finger. I pried it loose and wiped it on the rug.

And their live show. Astrampsychos hadn't even played. Poor A. Hex hadn't burst a single bass string, and they'd effectively neutered King Diamond, a veteran, an originator of all that is unholy.

The other band didn't concern me, though. Morbid Mastication. Splatter gore Carcass worship from some other Belgian town.

You could tell how they'd sound by the logo alone, smeary red letters shaped as therapy art by a criminally insane kindergartner. They'd sound like a copy of *Grey's Anat-*

omy shoved into a paper shredder. A morbid one.

Besides, I figured, as I dropped some cables and guitar pedals into my backpack, if Nekrokor hates us, he'll really hate them.

I zipped up my abiban jacket and resolved to make the best of it.

Then, the phone rang.

It cheeped its little Eurochirp that I always mistook for an alarm clock or a doorbell.

I figured it was Svart telling me to hurry up. I'd told him I'd be there at seven to help set up before they opened the doors, but that was over an hour ago. I can be unreliable when I'm nervous.

"Duude!" I said into the receiver, hoping to disarm his annoyance with a charming dose of American-style casual familiarity.

He didn't say anything, though. I just heard static, the faintest ghost syllables of a thousand other conversations.

"Hello?" I said again, slightly concerned. Svart's not the quiet type. Not if he's pissed off.

"Is that you, David?" a girl's voice asked.

"Ma . . ." I stopped. The voice was too high and smooth to be Maria's, her throat jagged by a thousand hand rolled cigarettes.

"It's me. Natasha." She practically whispered her name. I shivered.

"Natasha?" Something rumbled in my gut. The guilt I called by her name.

Even though I'd been dreading the show, right then I wanted nothing more than to drop the phone, flee my place, and run to the club. I wanted every last iota of escapism the gods of heavy metal could shower down on me. Anything to avoid dealing with this. With her. Emotions.

"I saw your sister," she said. "At Publix. She offered to give me your number."

"Hunh," I grunted.

My sister. I bet she did, I thought.

She hated Natasha, called her Princess Jasmine. Like in *Aladdin*. I once made the mistake of saying something to her about Natasha's perfume. Nothing scandalous. Just that I liked it. That my girlfriend smelled good. From then on, my sister could never resist the urge to make some kind of joke about it. Last year, she gave me a two-pound bag of jasmine potpourri for Christmas.

It only made sense that she'd give Natasha my number as a way to fuck with me from across the open sea. She hated Natasha. And she loved for me to struggle.

"I got your postcard," she said.

"Cool," I said. Then, after some silence, "I got yours, too."

We went on this way for some time. Dancing around the main issue.

I looked at my watch. I was beyond late. A quarter past late. But I'd fantasized about a phone call like this for a long time.

"So," I started, "what do we do?"

Static.

"I don't know," she said.

"Can we be friends?" I asked. The static swallowed the echo of my voice. Somewhere in that transcontinental hiss, I heard the dim mumble of a man and woman speaking French.

"I don't think I could be friends with you," she said. More silence.

That started me on a stream of apologies. For the past. My poor treatment of her. All the things I did wrong. There may have been tears.

"I don't think I could be *just* friends with you," she said. "That's what I meant."

I thought of the guy. The hipster dude I'd seen her with. I wanted to know.

"Are you seeing anyone?" I asked.

"No," she said. More silence. Then, "Are you?"

"It's just me," I said. And I believed it somehow.

Just like I willed myself to believe what she said. That she wasn't seeing anyone. It could have been true.

Then, I tried to get off the phone. I felt like I'd made some grand purchase. Negotiated some impossible deal. It was like signing a record contract.

I needed to get away, process what we said. What it meant.

It took some more talking. More emotions. I promised to write her a letter. Call her soon. Eventually we hung up. Both of us at the same time.

I looked at my watch again, grabbed my stuff, and sprinted out of the apartment. I could only think one thing, one impossible mantra as I rode down the elevator: I'm back with Natasha. Long distance.

23.
Devour All Pretty Things

On the walk to the Frontline, I tried to put Natasha out of my mind. She was still so distant, just a voice. A series of long distance calls that would cost me money I didn't have. A series of long distance calls that wouldn't get me laid.

Like everything in Gent, I could get to the Frontline in fifteen minutes or so on foot, even hauling an unwieldy guitar case, a fact that never ceased to amaze me when I considered the hours I'd spent trapped in my car, frying in the torpor of Miami traffic.

I ran through the notes I'd play, impulsively drumming my fingers against my palm as I walked. The old nervous habit.

A cobblestone bridge crossed a wide canal at the end of my street. A boat festooned with beer banners and orange glowing lanterns bobbed in the water. Drinking students packed its deck, fore and aft. The boat bar. It floated at the outer fringe of the Overpoort party zone.

I'd taken Juan there once. Delphine came, too. But he'd been sullen that night. Unsteady on deck. At one point, he spilled his drink. Blamed it on the boat's barely discernible listing. I called him a landlubber. Delphine didn't know the word. She asked him what it meant and he just said, "Something stupid."

I should have known better. He hadn't even worn his piratical head wrap, opting instead for the top hat and overcoat. Gothic vampires heed not the call of the wretched sea.

As I walked across the bridge, I ran through the set list for the show. All *Infernö* tracks. Even "Winterminion Ensorcels." It ended with our newest song. Our weirdest song. The goat song.

Mathias called it "Cursed Shades of Orcus." He'd named everything we'd made since he joined the band. He said he'd taken the name and the lyrics from an ancient poem, "something old, something rotten." They had a depth beyond the cartoonish violence of Desekration's previous masterworks.

It wasn't a complicated song. A single riff repeated to the breaking point. To the point that, even to the guy playing it, you'd wonder if something was stuck. A scratched record. A stalled disc. The riff repeated, a simple series of notes sequenced through a tremolo blur, with the same sequence, but at higher octaves, gradually added to the mix.

Mathias wrote it, he said, on his keyboard. My keyboard, really. Around that droning pair of notes he'd played in my apartment. He'd designed the riff, the song, the repetition, to unsettle you. The notes, at higher and higher pitches, burrowed into your body. It made you sick of the notes. Of the body so weak it couldn't bear the notes. It made you sick and Nordikron's sick voice grated along with the notes in a staccato serration.

Until it all stopped. Until it all opened up in the most bizarre way. The riff, the nekroshrieks, moved you through a tunnel and emerged into an empyrean realm of keyboards and clean singing. The opera voice. He'd used it before on

"The Inmost Sanctum." The first track of *The Intrapsychic Secret*. And a keyboard. His keyboard now. Washing over it all. On its most generic setting. Not the murky range of sounds and tones I'd spent days deliberating over and calibrating for Katabasis.

He'd convinced everyone else that he'd found it. That he'd uncovered the elusive goat song. He even persuaded Svart that the keyboard—and not the bass—held it all together, produced the necessary effect.

While he'd come up with something good—as much as it pains me to admit it, Juan was probably right to call him the most talented guy in the group—I remained unconvinced it was as freighted with mystic meaning as he wanted us to believe. To feel.

He let us sing, too. Juan and I. He gave us lines, then laughed as we ran through them, just as he directed, in our echoey death grunts. "Yes, that will do. That will show him," he cackled before he launched into a clearly sung rendition of our lines.

I hummed the riff as I passed the boat bar. "Curse upon you, cursed shades of Orcus, which devour all pretty things." I sang the lines—our little death chorus—in my closest approximation of Nordikron's clean voice. No one saw me. More importantly, no one heard me. Between each word, I listened to the water silently lapping the sides of the boat. The shimmering water reflected the pale sliver of a freezing moon.

The club lay at the end of an alley that connected to Overpoortstraat. Directly across the street from the club, a gray concrete studentplex loomed like some Soviet ministry. A black iron gate swarmed with locked bikes flanked the street.

Goat Song Sacrifice

A yard planted with stunted trees separated the dormitory entrance and the gate. Small groups of Erasmus students, European exchange students, many speaking Spanish, moved through the dorm building's bright sliding doors and toward the clubs along the main drag, as if transported by some disco-powered conveyor belt. I thought I recognized a few of them from the language school. Maybe they'd sign up for Dutch level two? The yellow bikes plastered like cheap handbills across every flat surface were rentals, like mine.

The yard looked empty, except for something that, at first glance, I took for a decorative boulder, until I noticed that it shifted in the breeze.

I headed up the street, then stopped. The voyeur in me gazed a bit more intently. I thought I could make out a couple, entwined in an embrace, kind of half standing, half sitting. A bit too cold for an outdoor interlude. And early. Can anybody really be so wasted at 8 pm that they can't make it back to the studentenkamer?

Looking again, I thought they were two chicks. A blonde and a brunette. Two heads of long hair bumping, bumping. Blond and bruin, like the two flavors of Leffe on tap at the Frontline. I'd love to devour those pretty things, I thought, then headed up the street. I doubted my night would end in a post-concert triumphal boning on the dormitory yard. Maria had already told me she couldn't make it to the show. Besides, Natasha. Hadn't I renounced any more Euroboning?

My fantasies receded as I stepped toward the club. A fog of tobacco smoke shrouded the air as the Gentian metal contingent huddled in small groups around the door. They'd look over. Not all at once. But they all gauged the same things. They checked out my guitar case, plain except for a faded Plutonic Records sticker. They checked out the plain black work shoes I wore every day. They checked out the abiban jacket zipped to my neck, the four stripes down the sleeves. And then they looked away. I invited no additional consideration. They could tell I wasn't in Astrampsychos.

You could gauge the crowd, too. By their shirts. No one else had on a jacket. Unless it was denim and covered with patches or leather and studded with spikes. Nothing designed for warmth. You read the shirts and figured out what kind of crowd you'd got. At first glance, it looked like a fairly standard assortment: some Carcass shirts, some Napalm Death shirts, some Deicide shirts. You could switch this crowd with any group of Floridian metal miscreants out for a night at the Button South and no one would know the difference.

A pack of Erasmus students stumbled past. The guys, in crisp white shirts, necks open, collars popped, leaned into the slight, waifish girls they guided to the clubs. I'd hate to have to walk through this gauntlet to go to a stupid disco.

As I got closer to the door, I passed a few guys repping old Belgian bands. An Ostrogoth shirt, like Maria's. A Warhead hat. And a lot of younger kids, too. In newer shirts. Lintless. Still creased. Emblazoned with the Astrampsychos sigil and the cosmic pentagram on *The Intrapsychic Secret*. The back had a phrase, "He who is, and was, and always shall be," from "The Inmost Sanctum."

Flyers for the show plastered the door. An enormous "A" dripped red across the door like the tendrilled blob of a whale's cyst.

One of the Astrampsychos kids, he couldn't have been more than sixteen, turned to me and said something in Dutch. I stared back. He switched to English. They learn that trick early. He said, "You ready to see the best band in the world?"

I just shook my head and pushed through the door. He

188

didn't mean Desekration. Hadn't he seen my guitar?

Inside, a bare chested Tomi sat on the stage in front of his drum kit. He had on gray sweatpants and high tops. The stage barely reached my knee. It seemed like a perfect set up for a puppet theatre troupe, but that's about it.

A pair of tiki torches stood on either side of the drums. The kind with little faux bamboo shafts. My sister always kept a few of these on hand to keep the mosquitoes away as her lame friends swilled Bud Lights on summer nights. Toward the back of the stage, my old keyboard sat on top of a stack of amps.

"Hey Tomi," I said. "Hoe gaat het? Where's everyone else?"

He gazed up from screwing the top bolt onto the cymbals. He stared at me for a second too long before answering, his words, as usual, swimming slowly. His word.

"Upstairs."

Then he went back to work.

I pushed through the crowd to get to the stairs. A crowd made up almost uniformly of kids in brand new Astrampsychos shirts. More than a few of them with corpsepaint-caked faces.

Upstairs in a bland tan room, Svart stooped over a table as he brushed on black fingernail polish. A dainty bottle of Cover Girl Onyx sat next to a plastic cup of beer. He dipped into the polish three or four times per nail and dribbled inky puddles across the table each time he reapplied.

Bullet belted and corpsepainted, he had on the complete "To Winds ov Demise" kit. Juan stood across the table, his face a picture of undead agony from beneath the brim of his top hat. A fine tinge of his animal funk drifted beneath the nail polish vapor. He splayed his painted fingers well away from his trench coat and slowly flapped his hands to dry

189

them.

A mass of junk lay piled in the middle of the table between them. Lengths of chain, armbands of various widths and spikiness, a jumble of chicken bones, as well as helmets and weapons. I spotted a fencing rapier, a camping hatchet, and a Nerf mace coated in silver Rustoleum. The grim war gear of a Geatish garage sale.

"What's all this shit?" I asked, but I knew the answer. We were going to play in costume. Someone expected it. Maybe Nordikron. Maybe Nekrokor. Maybe everyone but me expected it. Everyone but me and Tomi. But no one cares what the drummer wears.

"This show is going to be nekro," Juan said. He flashed the horns. He'd never done that before. Each nail shone with a glossy finish.

I put down my stuff and unzipped my jacket before rooting around in the pile. As long as they don't make me wear a nametag, I thought.

A heavily studded armband seemed like the obvious choice, so I pulled one on and felt cool for about five seconds. Its porcupine quills conveyed an unapproachable toughness that I rarely felt in real life. But as soon as I fastened it, the nails brushed continuously against my skin and their tips poked my hips. I had to bow my arms in a Hulk Hogan stance unless I wanted an ongoing acutreatment.

I took it off and tried to pry out some of the nails. Each armband had about sixty. But then Svart pointed the fingernail polish brush at me and said, "Don't fuck with that! Those things are expensive!"

So I just set it down and picked up the mass of chicken bones. A thin layer of grease coated the purplish brown bones, an assortment of thighs, wings, and drumsticks. They'd been joined together with two strands of fishing wire.

Goat Song Sacrifice

I figured Svart made it as another armband and that its cash value was about equal to a rotisserie chicken minus the meat.

I figured he'd made it as an armband, but when I put it around my arm, it immediately slipped to the ground. Svart finished his fingernails and gulped down his beer. I picked up the armband, then held the thing up to gauge its size. I settled it on my head like an ivory tiara.

"Ha ha!" Svart laughed, then grunted at Juan, "Hey, he's finally learning. You owe me a beer. You said he wouldn't wear any of this stuff."

Juan carefully reached into his coat—he didn't want to ruin his fingernail finish—and pinched out a few little plastic chips, the drink tickets I'd encountered pretty regularly at Euroclubs. He tossed them onto the table.

If they had a bet, I wanted Juan to lose. So I dug back into the pile on the table, pulled out a thick chain—Svart's bike lock—and draped it across my chest. A kid's shin guard, lacquered silver like the Nerf mace, rested on top of a few jars of greasepaint. I pulled the shin guard on one wrist and haphazardly rubbed a few globs of white grease-paint onto my cheeks, across my nose, and over my fore-head. I topped it off with a daub of black beneath each eye, but sidewise, like some braindead football hero. It was my little joke. My silent protest.

Svart then handed me the tickets.

"I knew you could do it," he said. "Go get us some beers!"

191

I pocketed the drink tickets and headed to the bar, jostling through the growing crowd. On stage, Tomi, arms crossed, peered at his drums as if they were some abstruse installation art piece. Even though the crowd was thicker, it now parted easily for me. The kids in Astrampsychos shirts practically followed me to the bar, where the bartender served me immediately. Chicken bones will get you everywhere. Within minutes, I was back upstairs with beers for each of us.

"Where's Nordikron?" I asked. It was almost nine. "Don't we play soon?"

"We have time," Svart said. "Astrampsychos has cancelled."

I couldn't quite believe him. The posters. The hype. The shattered dreams of Belgian teens.

"Goathorn, their singer. He has not yet recovered."

"Oh." I remembered the blue hand dangling from the coffin.

Svart went on, evidently unaffected by the near asphyxiation he'd witnessed just a few weeks before.

"It is just as well. Torburn, their drummer, cannot play either. He's finally been diagnosed."

"Diagnosed?"

"His playing has been weak since Nordikron's departure. Nekrokor—he is here tonight. Everyone is here tonight. They're just not here to play. Nekrokor, he told me they presumed a hex. Several counter hexes later, and a whole goat boiled down to its dried bones, still no improving. And that is when the . . . Municipal Services Department intervened."

Juan cut in: "You've got to hear this."

"Yes. His injury interfered with his day job. He drives a garbage truck for the city. Not only could he no longer drum effectively, he could also not operate the truck's hydraulic lift.

The physical therapist concedes it to be a . . ." He looked over at Juan. "How do you call it?"

"A rotator cuff. A torn rotator cuff."

"Fuck." I thought of Tomi on his way to spinning class. "Good thing our guy works out. Nekrokor's here?"

I felt lightheaded, nervous. They key advantage of my nekrocostume, I figured, was that I could blend in.

"Yah," Svart chuckled. "And you're not the only one who should worry. Isn't that right, Juan? You best to play good, or he'll take her back."

This set Juan off. He stamped in little circles around the room, his voice high pitched and screechy.

"He dated her, that asshole. He broke her heart and abused her. I knew some guy had damaged her. We've spent many nights talking about it. I just didn't know it was him—that asshole—until earlier tonight."

Svart pulled out a pack of bass strings.

"You'd better keep an eye on her, my friend. The fat ones," he leered. "They are always—how do you say?—'hot to trot.'"

"Oh dude," I said. "I tried to tell you. Remember? That day at your place. He was with her."

"I'm not a child," Juan said. "I knew they had a past. I just didn't realize he was the guy that . . ."

He took a deep breath, then said in a small voice, "She just wanted to talk to him that day. She wanted closure."

"Hmm. Closure? More like she wanted klote." Svart jabbed my shoulder with his fist and made an obscene gesture.

Balls. Svart taught me that one on our earliest drinking mission.

Juan sat down, defeated, and fiddled with the rapier on the table.

Svart explained that they'd seen Nekrokor earlier as they unloaded Tomi's drum kit from the car. Delphine had tagged along with Juan.

"I wanted her along," Svart said. "I knew she'd pull her weight. Ha ha! But then Nekrokor came by. Before I knew it, she disappeared. Him, too. That was in the afternoon. They didn't come back for a long time."

"Did you see her leave?" I asked Juan.

"He was inside helping Tomi," Svart said. "He missed it."

"Is that other band still playing?" I asked. I felt bad for Juan.

"Yes. Morbid Mastication now headlines," Svart said.

He looked up at a clock on the wall and scowled: "They will arrive by midnight at the earliest. They are Walloons."

Then, to clarify, "French speakers. They should not belong to Belgium."

"Oh," I sipped the beer. "So we have a few hours then. Until we play."

Svart said, "No. That is not done. Go and find Mathias."

"How should I know where he is?" I asked.

Svart shrugged, then pulled his bass out of its case.

"He may be inside. Or he may be outside. He said something about going out. Uitgaan. Or maybe it was to dig? Uitgraven. Hard to tell sometimes, with his accent."

I took my beer and headed back downstairs. Fully assembled, Tomi's drum kit engulfed most of the stage. He stood to the side, twirling two drumsticks, then raising his arms above his head. He sprinted in place and gripped the drumsticks like relay batons. He would never break, not like Torburn.

I felt the urge to bring him a sports drink, a cool Glucozade to reward his proactive fitness, and went over to see if he needed a beer. That's when I heard Delphine. Over by the bathrooms. Her burly tenor overpowered the combined voices of the crowd. She had some guy blocked in a corner. Peering around her girth, I spied Nekrokor standing calmly, his hand in her palm.

Just then, the club shook with an insistent rumble. It drowned out everything, even Delphine's voice. Tomi had finished his calisthenics. He sat behind the kit and put the double bass through its paces.

The sound renewed my anxiety; my heart pounded to match Tomi's pace. And I couldn't find Nordikron anywhere. More and more people packed the club. The cold night air blew in through the open door. Outside, I thought. He must be outside. I pushed through a group of guys by the door. One held his hands up to me like I was some kind of faith healer. He touched my hair. My bone crown, too.

The street was nearly empty. Even the flow of study abroad clubbers had slowed to a trickle. Doors at eight, show at nine. That Belgian punctuality, I thought, at work and at play. It infected everything, everyone.

Or at least everyone but Nordikron. I scanned the block again, and caught a flicker of motion from the yard fronting the student residence hall. Was that couple I'd seen still out there? Still at it? An impossible thought dawned on me. Could it be Nordikron out there, playing in the dark? Giving it away to some Satanic groupie? I dashed through the gate and onto the grass with the zeal of an Olympic sprinter. This I had to see.

He was there, alright. The scalloped edges of his cape brushed the ground. He was alone beneath a canopy of two trees, bent at the waist, his back to me. I stepped closer, heard a deep breathing. The hunched back beneath the cape expanded and contracted. Was he stroking off?

The metal gate creaked behind me. A shadow hovered down the street on a rusty bike. Nordikron still stood there, stooped over. I smiled, took a sip of beer, and waited for a minute, just enjoying the moment. My anxiety faded with each strained breath. It was like the opposite of Tomi's drum check. If he wasn't stroking, he had to be hyperventilating or something. I felt like I'd won. I finally had something over this hemophiliac little Nosferatu, discovered a chink in his impenetrably bizarre persona.

I didn't mean to chuckle, but must have. Nordikron turned, clutching a plastic bag to his mouth with a solid two-handed grip. There he was, the Satanic asthmatic. What a joke. The bag billowed like a balloon with his even breathing. And that's when I noticed something was wrong.

Even breathing. Not spastic at all. Over the edge of his clutched fists, his eyes gleamed with a radiant calm, as though he had just downed one of his clotted little vials. Flecks of mud, sodden leaves, bits of twig, covered his hands. A vicious stench, like an evil and bilious fart, blasted through the air, propelled as he turned to face me. Patches of dirt speckled Nordikron's cape, his pants, and his shirt, which must have been white at one point, but reflected a dismal gray pallor. Holes of various sizes, smeared grime, speckled lipid daubs, accessorized the shirt like Jackson Pollock polka dots. He stood in a pile of dirt, his boots straddling a shoe-box-sized hole in the ground.

The faint impression of a bent wing poked against the plastic bag. Nordikron inhaled deeply and stepped toward me. I could see a partially opened beak, the gray bubble of a dead eye. The odor hung beneath the branches like an evil miasma. I could see the ashen spaghetti of its vitals.

He moved the bag from his mouth and smiled.

"Is that . . .?" I asked.

"A sparrow?" He held up the bag and looked at it, the way you might look at a goldfish you'd just bought at a pet store. "From the park by your apartment." He gestured to my bone crown. "I see you've found its mate. The small, foolish birds can't understand how I attract, how I tempt them."

And as I covered my face, breathed through my mouth in shallow bursts, he moved his body close to mine, his head even closer, and lashed his tongue out at me so fast I couldn't help starting back.

"I must taste the stench of death before I perform."

He put the bag—the bird—in his cape.

"Let us go. I am ready."

Before I could respond, he'd pushed through the gate. He left me standing there under the trees, holding a beer, my feet at the edge of a little grave.

24.
With the Gleam of Tiki Torches

Nordikron disappeared into the club. He left dirt clumps, muddy footprints, in his wake. The few smokers still lingering on the sidewalk stubbed out their cigarettes and followed him in.

I stood in front of the door, in front of the red, globby "A," and slammed the rest of my beer.

"Let's do this," I said in the most self-motivational tone I could muster, then went inside.

The tiki torches blazed on either side of the stage. A black banner with the Desekration logo and Juan's drawing hung behind it. The sign of *Infernö*.

The crowd parted as Nordikron headed to the microphone stand at the center of the stage. A white hat or something hung over the mic.

Dozens of hands covered him and pushed him onto the stage. As he stood, he took out his bird bag and inhaled a few times like some wastoid huffing Freon. Then he threw the bag into the crowd.

He might as well have tossed it into a piranha pool. Within moments, bird parts, this wing, that wing, an indiscernible mass of feathers and flesh, moved across the crowd, passed from hand to hand to hand.

Everyone else was already on stage. Tomi sat behind his kit, his drumsticks resting on his thighs. To the left, Svart loomed like a granite statue. On the right, Juan stood with his back turned. As I neared the stage, I saw that he was helping Nekrokor with the keyboard. It was a guy with a guitar strapped over a black robe, but I knew it was Nekrokor—it was the same robe he had on at the Astrampsychos show.

I scanned the stage and found my guitar over by Svart. It was sitting on a stand and already plugged in. Glad someone's looking out for me, I thought, then made my way over to it. I strapped it on. Svart nudged me and pointed at a set list taped to the floor. I nodded. We'd decided on the set list at our last practice. Everything looked the same, except it now said "Intro" at the top.

I pointed to it with my toe, then shrugged. He gestured with his chin over to the synthesizer, where Nekrokor, his head shrouded in a cowl, stood with his fingers curled over the keys.

Nordikron pulled the hat hanging from the mic stand and held it above his head. It wasn't a hat; it was a white mask with a nose that drooped like a beluga's flaccid boner. It was the mask in Juan's drawing. It was the mask of the plague doctor. Nordikron put on the mask and the stage went dark except for one green light shining directly on him.

I guess that was Nekrokor's keyboard cue. He started to play. The Intro to Desekration's first live show, the aural storm of *Infernö*, took the unlikely form of a children's song. It took the form of "Ring Around the Rosie," dinging through the PA in dulcet Casio tones and accompanied by Nordikron in a lackadaisical nasal drone:

Ring around the rosie,
Pocket full of posies,
Ashes, ashes,
We all fall down.

He held the mic in his hand and spun in a small circle as he sang. When he got to the last line, he dropped to the stage and lay completely still, face down, his arms and legs a sprawled heap. Nekrokor plonked through the song once again, but Nordikron didn't move until it finished.

Then, Svart tapped me with his elbow and nodded. We started into the first song on the list and Nordikron immediately leaped from the floor with the sudden force of a reanimated corpse. He cupped the mic to his face, just below the long plague nose, and screamed, "Anno Yersinia Pestis Spiritus" in his most glass-gargled voice. In the year of our spiritual plague. It was the first line of *Infernö*'s title track.

The kids closest to the stage erupted in contorted paroxysms as if they, too, were plague corpses jerked back into the realm of the living.

Well, you know. Someone up front taped it with a giant camcorder the shape and color of an AT-AT walker. Just for themselves. It's on the internet now. The bottom corner time stamped from a receding age, a previous century. The image of the stage, of Desekration's first live show, grainy and lined by VHS decay.

People still watch it. Over 50,000 views. Even though most of it shows a greenish screen punctuated by swatches of fuzz. Even though the sound resembles a garbage disposal clogged with forks.

It sounded like that at the time, too. As I played. Something was wrong with my guitar. I noticed it as soon as I started playing. My lower strings flapped and wobbled more than they ever had in the depth of their deepest death metal downtune. At first I chalked it up to an accident, an unnecessary jostling when Svart, or maybe Juan, moved my guitar downstairs.

I figured I'd muddle through and retune before the next song. It was stupid of me not to check my guitar before playing. I mean, I hadn't really had time, but it was a mistake all the same. Still, no one would notice my discordant riffs through the club's muddy sound system and the pounding assault of Tomi's ongoing stormblast.

And then I tried to play the solo. It wasn't a hard one. Too tricky for Juan, but that doesn't mean much. It wasn't even a long solo. It wasn't some super technical heartwork that deserved its own title. It was a short, high-pitched animal shriek of a solo. The buzz saw of a goat's last bleat, of the blade across its neck. I stepped toward the front of the stage and flicked the highest string with my pick.

That's when I knew someone had sabotaged the guitar. If the lower strings flapped and farted like the loosest labia, the peg for the highest string had been tightened, tautened so much that the tip of my pick sliced right through the string. The popped string arced wildly and scratched my cheek.

I'd popped strings before, of course. It's unavoidable. When I played in Valhalla, it happened to me during a couple of gigs. It's the kind of thing that can throw you off, but it's not necessarily a disaster. I paused for a beat, then shifted to the next string. There's more than one way to play the solo, I figured. I could get the same notes by playing the lower string higher up the neck.

But then that string snapped, too. That's why people watch the video. To see what happened next. To see Nekrokor as he emerged from the other side of the stage with his guitar held high. To see Nekrokor as he played my solo, walked up to me, and then booted me square in the chest.

His heel ground Svart's bike lock into my sternum. I stumbled back.

He booted me a second time, then strummed the rest of my short solo. My feet hung past the edge of the stage.

The crowd, a wall of hands, buffeted me, but also held me steady.

Nekrokor then took his guitar and rammed its head into my chest. He rammed me off the stage. And into a bandless limbo.

Concluded in

SINISTER SYNTHESIZER

The Third Book
of the
Death Metal Epic

Dean Swinford is a novelist and English professor. His fiction includes *The Inverted Katabasis*, the first book of the *Death Metal Epic*, as well as work that has appeared in *The Café Irreal*, *Despumation*, and *The Healing Monsters*. He is also the author of *Through the Daemon's Gate*, a study of Johannes Kepler's *Somnium*. His essays have appeared in journals and edited collections including *Studies in Medievalism*, *Modern Philology*, *The Journal of Medieval Religious Cultures*, *Classical Traditions in Science Fiction*, *The Irreal Reader*, and *Kafka's Creatures*. He lives in North Carolina.

Other **Atlatl Press** Books

Come Home, We Love You Still by Justin Grimbol

We Did Everything Wrong by C.V. Hunt

Squirm With Me by Andersen Prunty

Hard Bodies by Justin Grimbol

Arafat Mountain by Mike Kleine

Drinking Until Morning by Justin Grimbol

Thanks For Ruining My Life by C.V. Hunt

Death Metal Epic (Book One: The Inverted Katabasis)
by Dean Swinford

Fill the Grand Canyon and Live Forever by Andersen Prunty

Mastodon Farm by Mike Kleine

Fuckness by Andersen Prunty

Losing the Light by Brian Cartwright

They Had Goat Heads by D. Harlan Wilson

The Beard by Andersen Prunty

Printed in Great Britain
by Amazon